Floating Islands

Joyce Mansour

translated by Emilie Moorhouse

INVISIBLE BOOKS

Halifax | Picton | Saint John

Library and Archives Canada Cataloguing in Publication

Title: Floating islands / Joyce Mansour ; translated by Emilie Moorhouse.
Other titles: Histoires nocives. English
Names: Mansour, Joyce, 1928-1986, author. | Moorhouse, Emilie, translator.
Description: Translation of: Histoires nocives. | Includes bibliographical references. | In English, translated from the French.
Identifiers: Canadiana (print) 20260225649
Canadiana (ebook) 20260226432
ISBN 9781778430916 (softcover)
ISBN 9781778430923 (EPUB)
Subjects: LCGFT: Short stories.
Classification: LCC PQ2673.A5 H4713 2026 | DDC 843/.914—dc23

Edited by Mélissa Bull and Maxime Raymond Bock
Cover design by CHIPS
Interior design by Megan Fildes

This translation was co-produced in the context of "Surreal Continuum" at Haus der Kulturen der Welt (HKW) in Berlin, in cooperation with EXC 2020 Temporal Communities.

Invisible Books is committed to protecting our natural environment. As part of our efforts, both the cover and interior of this book are printed on acid-free 100% post-consumer recycled fibres.

Printed and bound in Canada.

Invisible Books | Halifax, Picton, Saint John
www.invisiblebooks.ca

Published with the generous assistance of the Canada Council for the Arts, the Ontario Arts Council, and the Government of Canada.

Canada Council for the Arts Conseil des Arts du Canada ONTARIO ARTS COUNCIL CONSEIL DES ARTS DE L'ONTARIO an Ontario government agency un organisme du gouvernement de l'Ontario Canada

TRANSLATOR'S INTRODUCTION

"No one knows the face of their own death.
Mine has let her hair grow..."

Joyce Mansour (1928–1986) was a Syrian-Jewish and Anglo-Egyptian post-war Surrealist writer who settled in Paris after her exile from Egypt and whose work intertwines desire, violence, and transformation while blurring the boundaries between language and the body. While she is generally known for her poetry, this volume gathers three of her most significant stories, including "Floating Islands," her final work of narrative prose, an art form she never returned to in the fifteen years between its publication and her death. Together, these works span the full twenty years of her prose oeuvre.

Before this decade began, Mansour's work was difficult to find in English translation, and even more so in the original French. I encountered her poetry in the midst of the #MeToo movement going viral, as I was searching for an author to focus on for a translation workshop. When I realized most of her books were out of print, I became determined to bring her work the recognition it deserved. Now, as an increasing number of Mansour translations are being published and picked up by readers, my concern has shifted from the risk of her work being forgotten to a more subtle one: that it may be misrepresented or softened, her brilliance rendered more palatable and less threatening. In his 1985 monograph *Joyce Mansour*, J.H. Matthews observes:

> To speak of Joyce Mansour as a writer whose chief aim is to shock or infuriate the bourgeoisie would be a distortion of the inspiration behind her work and a perversion of the meaning behind some of the most remarkable Mansourian poems... The poetry of Mansour is strange, that is, it's written by a stranger, by a person drawing from a culture whose mythology is neither French, nor Greco-Roman... Mansour is not referring to ancient Egyptian mythology to shine in front of her colleagues or her readers. Rather her ambition is completely different: she wants to breathe in a world where the air is becoming unbreathable.

If one agrees with Matthews that Mansour's poetry is strange, they will find her prose nearly feral. Nowhere is Mansour's "need to breathe" more apparent than in this collection of fiction. Across these three tales, she draws on Surrealist strategies—dislocation, reversals, metamorphosis, and the breakdown of bodily boundaries—to expose and dismantle the suffocating limits imposed on women's identities, bodies, and desires.

These binaries and boundaries—active masculine and passive feminine, fertile life and abject death, acceptable and unacceptable desires, pleasure and pain, apes and humans (or gods), doctors and patients—are deeply embedded in Western patriarchal norms as a method of cementing who can wield power and who must be subject to it.

Transformation is persistent in Mansour's writing. Any attempt to fix her with a single label—Syrian, Egyptian, Jewish, Arab, daughter, widow, exile, European, Anglophone, wife, Francophile, mother, colonial bourgeois, anti-colonial Parisian Surrealist, poet, or artist—misses the complexity of her hybrid identity and underestimates how deeply her work is shaped by bilingualism, code-switching, and linguistic reversals.

With Mansour, freedom comes through desire, sex, and death—destruction as reinvention; figures change form, cross genders, cross species, suffer, die, and are reborn without judgement or exile. This mutability gives Mansour room to imagine liberation not through purity or restraint, but through continual metamorphosis. Mansour's need to breathe is thus a need for a space in which the self can fully unfold, where desire, as a gateway to the unconscious and to social disruption, is no longer shameful but a force for liberation of a shifting self.

Born Joyce Patricia Adès in 1928 in Bowden, UK, near Manchester, Mansour moved with her family to Cairo in infancy, where the Adès family business was based. Mansour, "born into a life of splendour, opulence, and pomp," grew up within Cairo's cosmopolitan elite. The Adès family, "a cornerstone of Egypt's Jewish community,"[1] were major figures in commerce and high society, found-

1 Saleh.

ing Les Grands Magasins Adès and playing a key role in the Egyptian textile industry. Raised in a Sephardic Jewish household, Mansour spoke Ladino—a Romance language mixing medieval Spanish with Hebrew, Turkish, Greek, and Arabic—in her early years but was formally educated in English. "Suddenly," said Mansour, "I began to think in English, the first language I had understood despite the illiterate Spanish-Arabic-Yiddish environment of my young years."[2]

Two great losses marked Mansour's early life. In 1944, when Mansour was fifteen, her mother died of cancer. In 1947, after returning from a prolonged European honeymoon with her first husband, Henri Naggar, he too died of cancer. Mansour was eighteen. Her bereavement, set against the backdrop of WWII and the Shoah, utterly consumed her. She locked herself away, cut off almost entirely from her social circle, and refused to see even her father. Suffering from night terrors and somnambulism, she accepted only the company of her sister-in-law, with whom she lived. It was at this point that she began to write. Plunged into a deep depression, she turned to poetry to cope, to "remove the blood from [her] dreams."[3] Her first lines were "improvised poems in the bathtub. Alone, she would talk, scream as though to cover the sound of the water. It was a kind of revolt."[4] Mansour penned her first poems in English.

2 Author's translation of: "Soudain je me mis à penser en anglais, la première langue que j'eusse comprise en dépit de l'entourage analphabète hispano-arabo-yiddish de mes jeunes années." (Mansour, "Illusions de vol," 73.)

3 Author's translation of: "d'effacer le sang de ses rêves." (Missir, 20.)

4 Author's translation of: "Elle disait qu'elle avait commencé par improviser des poèmes dans la baignoire. Seule, elle parlait, criait pour couvrir le bruit de l'eau. C'était une sorte de révolte." (Missir, 20.)

She later described them as "crazed with rage... exclusively insults... In fact, no one has ever seen them."[5] These early writings have never been found.

In 1948, when Mansour was nineteen, she met her second husband, Samir Mansour, a wealthy, French-educated Egyptian banker and businessman. The couple married in 1949 and would go on to have two sons together, dividing their time between Cairo and Paris. Mansour's marriage to Samir profoundly impacted her life and work. It was with him that she began to live, to think, and to write in French, the language of nearly all her published writing. "I met a man," she said, "who refused to speak anything but French. So, I gave up English and started reading, writing, and trying to think in French. I began a new life with new thoughts. When I reread the things I had written in English, they were completely different, as if someone else had come along at that moment."[6]

Joyce and Samir Mansour were still living in Cairo when her first collection of poetry, *Cris*, was published in 1953. Later recognized as a seminal text in postwar Surrealism, *Cris*, with its focus on death, sex, decomposing bodies, and shifting identities, unsettled her high society connections in Egypt. Mansour sent André Breton a copy of *Cris* the year it was published. They would eventually form a very close friendship that lasted until Breton's death, with Mansour dedicating much of her work to him. Mansour, already ac-

5 Author's translation of: "Ce que j'écrivais était fou de rage, fou... c'est vrai. C'était uniquement des injures. Ça à l'air d'une blague, mais c'était totalement injurieux. Personne ne les a vus d'ailleurs." (Missir, 20.)

6 Author's translation of: "J'ai rencontré un homme qui refusait de parler autre chose que le français. Alors, j'ai laissé tomber l'anglais et je me suis mise à lire, à écrire, à essayer de penser en français. J'ai commencé une nouvelle vie avec de nouvelles pensées. Quand j'ai relu les choses que j'écrivais en langue anglaise, ça n'avait rien à voir, comme si quelqu'un d'autre était venu à ce moment." (Missir, 21.)

quainted with Cairo's Surrealist luminary Georges Henein, was soon the toast of the French literati "who found in her poetry a stunning instance of what André Breton identified as the primary objective of art: to present revolutionary, liberating truths as experienced in the unconscious."[7]

When Gamal Abdel Nasser took power in Egypt (1952–1956) in a socialist revolution that deposed King Farouk I and ended seventy-five years of British occupation, Mansour's and the Adèses' family homes and assets were seized by the new government. Her father and brothers were jailed for one month, and in 1956 they were exiled to Switzerland. The Mansours left Cairo for Paris the same year.[8]

Once in France, Joyce and Samir Mansour found new footing. Embraced by the Paris Surrealists, Joyce Mansour befriended and worked alongside André Breton, André Pieyre de Mandiargues, Ted Joans, Wifredo Lam, and Alain Jouffroy, among other artists. The Mansours hosted Surrealist gatherings in their Paris apartment, including one instance in which they invited guests to view *L'exécution du testament du Marquis de Sade*, a performance piece by Jean Benoît. These friendships shaped Mansour's practice; she would go on to publish sixteen books of poetry and multiple works of fiction and theatre, all in French.

The second story in this collection, "Julius Caesar," Mansour's earliest published work of literary fiction, appeared in 1955 (with a cover illustration by the German Surrealist Hans Bellmer), while Mansour was still living in Egypt. Its

7 Mambrol.

8 Missir, 44.

protagonist, Julius Caesar, a Black wet nurse to twin boys, tries to contain their mounting obsessions with carnal knowledge and divine wisdom. As their Alpine community readies haphazardly for a flood to rival Noah's, Julius Caesar is the sole remaining character to board a makeshift raft and escape the rising floodwaters.

Set in the Swiss Alps, "Julius Caesar" blends graphic dystopian biblical narratives with ancient Egyptian mythology—including references to Hathor and Babi—as well as lewd fairytale tropes and reinvented, carnivalesque hagiographies. In this epic tale, characters chase sex, death, prey, and glory. They search for God (or gods), but the only one they meet is a giant ape lured to their location by the scent of a scrap of the beguiling Lucie the virgin's clothing. (The object of the twins' amorous intentions, Lucie's charactonym is not truly indicative of her sexual inexperience.) Said Mansour of writing "Julius Caesar": "The things I put into 'Julius Caesar,' I felt them, I dreamed of them, I knew them. Most of them are dreams, but some characters were inspired by people I knew."[9]

"The Parrot," a gut-punch of a short, violent fable steeped in distorted religious imagery and charged with sexual and animalistic excess, was published in its first iteration in the inaugural issue of André Breton's *Le Surréalisme, même* (1956). However, this first version of the encounter between Marie and the assassin was omitted from both editions of Mansour's French collected works, which instead included a significantly expanded text titled "Marie, ou l'honneur de servir," published in 1958. The earlier version of "Le per-

9 Author's translation of: "Les choses que j'ai mises dans Jules César, je les ai senties, j'en ai rêvé, je les ai connues. La plupart sont des rêves, mais certains personnages m'ont été inspirés par des gens que j'ai connus." (Desvaux-Mansour, 275.)

roquet" is the one featured in this translated collection. The subsuming, sexualized violence in this story—replete with mangled genitals, orifices, and, as expected from the title, a parrot—is at times brutal to read, in part due to the protagonist's active consent to her own submission and destruction. Is it a critique of the latent sadism of patriarchal interpretations of Judeo-Christian narratives? Of the violence concealed within the language of "service" and devotion reserved for women? It is both and more: a relentless dissection of the structures that sanctify feminine submission and make self-erasure appear virtuous. Against a contemporary backdrop in which "Biblical womanhood" is invoked to convince women to embrace complete submission to their husbands, what once read as surrealist provocation now reads as an unmasking.

"Floating Islands," published in 1973, is perhaps Mansour's most personal and groundbreaking work, serving as a kind of literary testament as it was her last work of narrative prose. Mansour, whose literary inspiration emerged in the aftermath of the deaths of her mother and first husband and was shaped by repeated visits to dying loved ones in hospital, closes the loop in "Floating Islands" by returning to the hospital more than twenty years later to visit her father. Deploying a large cast of cantankerous characters, the story, set primarily in a Geneva hospital, explores physical and mental illnesses, unruly desires, otherworldly dreamscapes, extended institutionalizations, and, of course, death. Written as Mansour visited her dying father, "Floating Islands" plunges readers into the swilling, viscous realm of the corporeal—at times pleasurable, often horrific, disturbingly erotic, or absurd (interchangeably and simultaneously so). As Jean Chalon wrote in a 1973 review in the conservative-leaning newspaper *Le Figaro*: "These are the realities of a Swiss hospital as seen by the last of the Surrealists... A long nightmare full of automatic obscenities, stenches, and depravities."[10]

A stylistic tour-de-force, the collection of vignettes (or literary islands) is recounted from shifting perspectives—sometimes in the first person singular ("a dead leaf falls on my mouth"), others in the second person ("on a bench, you listen to a conversation between doctors") and first person plural ("we say, 'Open the parentheses.'"). With these pronoun shifts, Mansour situates the self as one among a larger collective—or a chorus of selves—and reveals an 'I' that is not exempt from role reversals. In a conversation between a doctor and a cancer patient, the doctor acknowledges that he too will be a patient someday: "As a doctor I should try to carve you up; but as a man, or better yet, as a future patient, I understand your position." Mansour collapses the boundaries that separate us—boundaries that sustain dehumanization—and in doing so unsettles the idea of fixity itself: what seems stable is always shifting.

Throughout "Floating Islands," Mansour continually morphs her narrative selves, toying with the expected boundaries between the imagined "I," the "I" which navigates the "real" hospital where her "real" father is dying, and the "I" of her dreams. Each iteration of the first person is simultaneously identical yet also distinct. Through this fluid interplay of consciousnesses, Mansour embodies the principles set forth in Breton's 1932 *Les vases communicants*, namely, highlighting the communication between dreams

10 Author's translation of: "Ce dont les réalités d'un hôpital suisse vues par la dernière des surrealistes... Un long cauchemar plein d'obscénités automatiques, de puanteurs et de déchéances." (Chalon.)

and reality, the "surreality" of the quotidian, the reconciliation of action and dreams, the role of desire. In doing so, she blends materiality and imagination into a cyclical, non-linear continuum, dissolving Western culture's traditional hierarchies that privilege seemingly objective or logical realities above complex subjective experiences.

While Mansour's work remains as provocative and relevant as when it was first published, on occasion she employs certain outdated words worth addressing, particularly as they relate to race.

In my 2023 translation of Mansour's poetry, *Emerald Wounds*, my choice for one such word was questioned by critic Anahid Nersessian in the *New York Review of Books*. I had translated Mansour's use of *nègres* as "blacks." The reviewer suggested that my word choice was misleading as it might be hiding Mansour's racism: "It's hard to know what to make of Mansour's racial attitudes... When Mansour wrote *nègres* instead of *noirs*, did she mean to adopt what had, by mid-century, become the term of choice in many progressive circles? Or was she using *nègres* in a more colloquial sense, one that could include an outright hateful meaning?"

The answer to the questions posed by Nersessian depends very much on the context in which the word is used. Having carefully considered my word choice, especially in this instance, I responded to Nersessian, by highlighting the history of the word, and how it had been intentionally reclaimed more than a decade prior to Mansour's use of it in her work. "I felt that the English word that best reflected the intention of the poet was not an outdated term that would change the tone of the poem, but one that is more reflective of a modern reclamation like the one intended by her fellow Surrealist poet Aimé Césaire."[11]

Aimé Césaire and his wife Suzanne Césaire, both from Martinique, alongside Léon-Gontran Damas from French Guiana and Léopold Sédar Senghor from Sénégal, developed what became the Négritude movement, which reclaimed the somewhat ambiguous but mostly derogatory French word *nègre*, thus transforming a racist slur into a word of power, carrying the humanity, rage, and dignity, as well as the long legacy of the labour, of formerly enslaved Black people.

In *Cahier d'un retour au pays natal*, first published in 1939 and then republished in 1947 with a preface by André Breton and frontispiece by Wifredo Lam, Aimé Césaire flipped the colonial script and further imbued the term with empowerment and historical consciousness:

> Haïti, where Négritude stood up for the first time,
>   believing in her humanity [...]
>
> And I say Bordeau and Nantes and Liverpool and
>   New York and San Francisco
> not a single piece of this world is without my
>   fingerprints
> and my heel on the back of skyscrapers, and my filth
>   in the glitter of gems.
> Who can lay claim to more?

Césaire was not just reclaiming a single word, but an entire

11 Moorhouse.

history whose narrative had been monopolized by a white supremacist, colonial European worldview. This reversal is typical of Surrealists.

In "Julius Caesar," Mansour, by replacing a symbol of conquest and authoritarianism with the historically erased figure of a Black wet nurse, offers literature a new Julius Caesar: a Black woman who has nourished, with her own body, the ungrateful children in her charge.

I have translated *négresse*, the feminized French form of *nègre*, in this story as "Black," a choice I believe is both appropriate to Mansour's intention and better suited to our time and to our readership. It is my belief that her choice of this word in French, which occurs three times in the story to describe the main character, was meant as a condemnation of racist colonial attitudes. In fact, in "Floating Islands," in what is perhaps one of the most vitriolic passages of this entire book, Mansour spares no mercy for the hypocrisy and lies of national myths, namely those of Swiss "cleanliness," xenophobia, and chauvinism together disguised as respectability, and the mental and moral decay engendered by bigotry:

> I say with regret: the myth of Swiss cleanliness has a tough skin, but thanks to a pathetic and small caste of ultra-chauvinistic patients whose talk is peppered with racist scraps, the filth, hidden beneath ample Protestant skirts, lifts its head and sees the light of day.

This passage is followed by a quote from Antonin Artaud ("Calm as madmen") before Mansour turns her revulsion onto the most serene of targets: "I hate lac Léman." Artaud claimed that those institutionalized by society for "madness" were those who rejected society's crimes: "Society has strangled in its asylums all those whom it needed to get rid of, or protect itself from, for they refused to become complicit in its foulest deeds. For an institutionalized man is one whom society wants to silence, so as to prevent him from uttering unbearable truths."[12] For Artaud, the mad are calm because they are lucid. In expressing her hatred for the lake, Mansour is not soothed, but rather provoked by the misleading beauty of a tranquil landscape, as it so easily dupes the mind into forgetting human grotesqueness. In a book saturated with images of sickness, death, and bodily fluids, this passage condenses Mansour's rage and disgust into a single, cutting image: "The filth of ashtrays or chamber pots that are never fully emptied has no equal in my view than that of the grime of a badly stuffed mind." This kind of waste is never expelled, but internalized, lodged in a disturbed consciousness.

Mansour's citation of Artaud is one of many—her fiction unfolds as a constant intertextual conversation. "Marie, ou l'honneur de servir" ("Marie, or the Honour of Serving"), for example, recalls Sade's *Justine, ou les malheurs de la vertu*. *Le Bleu des Fonds (The Blue of the Depths)* alludes to Bataille's *The Blue of Noon*. While the title "Floating Islands" ("Îles flottantes") itself is not a reference to any specific work or author, scholar Marie Claire Dumas theorizes that because

12 Author's translation of: "C'est ainsi que la société a fait étrangler dans ses asiles tous ceux dont elle a voulu se débarrasser ou se défendre, comme ayant refusé de se rendre avec elle complices de certaines hautes saletés. Car un aliéné est aussi un homme que la société n'a pas voulu entendre et qu'elle a voulu empêcher d'émettre d'insupportables vérités." (Artaud, 7.)

its original French title is a play on words, it could be an allusion to multiple deceased authors: It's a traditional French dessert (with poached meringues adrift atop a sea of creamy vanilla custard), and it riffs on the French plural masculine pronoun *ils* or "they." As Dumas explains, aurally, *îles flottantes* suggests "floating theys," or several unidentified floating bodies. For Mansour, it's the dead who float—"we don't live with the dead... they float and tremble in the evening wind"—so the title might also be understood as "the floating dead guys."[13]

This intertextual conversation is sustained throughout "Floating Islands." The narrator opens by telling us she's reading Pierre Jean Jouve's *The Desert World*. Quoting heavily from the novel, the narrator inhabits multiple perspectives: reader, writer, and even various characters—books within books, worlds within worlds. Mansour herself seems to be merging with other writers' works to the point where the boundaries of whose words belong to whom grow porous.

The work's intertextuality is a fascinating meditation on the extent to which Mansour's own writing was influenced by other artists, their work woven into her subconscious, into her dreams. These literary interchanges reveal how the creative works of others shape our own ideas—to the point where we might mistakenly think we've independently come up with a new thought when in fact the idea was planted in our minds by someone else, by something we read, or by something we heard. To this point, Mansour's narrator interrogates whether citing Pierre Bourgeade is plagiarism: "I had completely forgotten that interview, and

13 Author's translation of: "On ne vit pas avec les morts... Ils flottent et tremblent dans le vent du soir." (Mansour, *Œuvres complètes*, 590.)

the dream, to the point of repeating it, image by image, without recognizing it belonged to another. Plagiarism or a bad joke?"[14]

Surrealism is often confused with the "unreal," which Naomi Klein describes as "the replacement of organic life with artifice" such as "a reality show star who becomes president of the United States" or a "heat wave in the Arctic."[15] Rather than replacing organic life with artifice, Mansour and the Surrealists were on a quest to reveal an absolute reality.

Recent world events are so destabilizing they haunt us with the impression we are living in an *unreal*—not surreal—time. But if we don't recognize the world in which we find ourselves, perhaps it's because we have spent too much time turning away from those things we find unpleasant and uncomfortable. As Jean-Louis Bédouin wrote in 1954, Mansour returns to the essential "in a time of pin-ups and cover-girls, in a time of learned ignorance about true human needs."[16] Mansour's often brutal fiction is a mirror: it compels us to engage with the things about ourselves we refuse to see, or prefer to hide. It shakes us from the false comfort of vanities, forcing us to own up to our unwitting roles in shaping this unrecognizable world—one mired in escalating climate crises, catastrophic violence, oppression, inequality, and ne-

14 Author's translation of: "J'avais totalement oublié le contenu de cette interview, le rêve également; au point de le répéter, image pour image, sans le reconnaître comme appartenant à un autre. Plagiat ou pantalonnade?" (Mansour, *Histoires nocives*, 70.)

15 Klein, "Surrealism Against Facism."

16 Author's translation of: "...Au temps des pin-up et des cover-girls, au temps de l'ignorance apprise des vraies nécessités humaines..." (Missir, 31).

glect. As our world tilts ever further into this abyss, Mansour's stories might serve as transgressive invocations, as flares to illuminate and name the grotesque carnival aspects of things for what they are. They invite us all to be bolder, to write and read and think in ways that are ungovernable.

Loss is what first compelled Mansour to write. With her attention on the sombre contradictions of her own life, Mansour flamed into a formidable, defiant force, surviving transformations she would not have chosen, discovering a community of collaborators within the Surrealist group who were equally uncompromising and ferocious. The resurgence of interest in Mansour's work now is not just of literary relevance. Surrealism at its best was a collective resistance to the narratives that trick us into accepting the limits placed on the most sincere and rebellious of human instincts—desire and imagination. Mansour understood this not as theory but as practice, as lived experience, as the only honest response to loss, exile, erasure, and institutionalized violence.

BIBLIOGRAPHY

Artaud, Antonin. *Van Gogh: Le suicidé de la société*. Paris, Gallimard, 1947. https://ebooks-bnr.com/ebooks/pdf4/artaud_van_gogh_suicide_societe.pdf

Breton, André. *Les Vases communicants*. Paris: Éditions des Cahiers libres, 1932.

Carruthers, Victoria. "Excessive Bodies, Shifting Subjects and Voice in the Poetry of Joyce Mansour," *Dada/Surrealism* 19, no. 1 (2013): 1–14.

Césaire, Aimé. "Cahier d'un retour au pays natal," *Volontés* 20, August 1939.

Césaire, Aimé. *The Original Notebook of a Return to the Native Land: Bilingual Edition*. Translated by Mireille Rosello and Annie Pritchard. Hexham: Bloodaxe Contemporary French Poets, 1995.

Chadwick, Whitney. *Women Artists and the Surrealist Movement*. London: Thames and Hudson, 2021.

Chalon, Jean. "Le parfum de la dame en noir," *Le Figaro*, March 31, 1973.

Diagne, Souleymane Bachir. "Négritude," *The Stanford Encyclopedia of Philosophy* (Spring 2023 Edition), Edward N. Zalta & Uri Nodelman (eds.). https://plato.stanford.edu/archives/spr2023/entries/negritude.

Domenick, Sarah. "'Mon rire vole haut:' Joyce Mansour and Black Humor," *Comparative Literature* M.A. Essays. Hanover: Dartmouth College Digital Commons, 2017. https://digitalcommons.dartmouth.edu/cgi/viewcontent.cgi?article=1165&context=complit_essays

Dumas, Marie Claude. "Îles flottantes: Où ils et elles parlent," *Littérature* no. 97, 1995: 64–72.

Elhariry, Yasser. "Divine Breath of Genesis (Joyce Mansour)" *Francosphères* 6, no. 1 (2017): 61–86.

Jouve, Jean. *The Desert World*. Translated by Lydia Davis. Marlboro, Vermont: Marlboro Press, 1996.

Klein, Naomi. "Surrealism Against Fascism," *Equator*, November 26, 2025. https://www.equator.org/articles/surrealism-against-fascism

Mambrol, Nasrullah. "Analysis of Joyce Mansour's Screams," Literariness, July 2, 2025. https://literariness.org/2025/07/02/analysis-of-joyce-mansours-screams/

Mansour, Joyce. "Illusions de vol," *Ça*. Paris: Le Soleil Noir, 1970.

Mansour, Joyce. *Carré blanc*. Paris: Le Soleil Noir, 1965.

Mansour, Joyce. *Cris*. Paris: Seghers, 1953.

Mansour, Joyce. *Emerald Wounds: Selected Poems*. Translated by Emilie Moorhouse. San Francisco: City Lights Books, 2023.

Mansour, Joyce. Joyce. *Histoires nocives: Jules César; Îles flottantes*. Paris: Gallimard, 1973.

Mansour, Joyce. *Jules César*. Paris: Seghers, 1955.

Mansour, Joyce. "Le Moyen-Orient et les livres: Jules César de Joyce Mansour." Interview. 1956. *Le surréalisme à travers Joyce Mansour: peinture et poésie, le miroir du désir* by Marie-Francine Desvaux-Mansour. PhD dissertation, Université Paris 1 Panthéon-Sorbonne, 2014.

Mansour, Joyce. "Le Perroquet." *Le Surréalisme, même*, no. 1 (October 1956): 13–15. Later reworked and published in *Les Gisants satisfaits* by Joyce Mansour. Paris: Jean-Jacques Pauvert, 1958.

Mansour, Joyce. *Œuvres complètes: Prose et Poésie*. Paris: Michel de Maule, 2014.

Mansour, Joyce. *Pandémonium*. Paris: La Nuova Foglio, 1975.

Mansour, Joyce. *Rapaces*. Paris: Seghers, 1960.

Mansour, Joyce. *Trous noirs*. Brussels: La Pierre d'Alun, 1986.

Matthews, J. H. *Joyce Mansour*. Amsterdam: Rodopi, 1985.

Missir, Marie-Laure. *Joyce Mansour: Une étrange demoiselle*. Paris: Jean-Michel Place, 2005.

Moorhouse, Emilie. "Letter to the Editors: Gray Area – In Response to Poems to Wake the Corpses." *The New York Review of Books,* October 19, 2023. https://www.nybooks.com/articles/2023/10/19/gray-area/

Nersessian, Anahid. "Poems to Wake the Corpses." *The New York Review of Books,* September 21, 2023. https://www.nybooks.com/articles/2023/09/21/poems-to-wake-the-corpses-joyce-mansour/

Saleh, Raïs. "The Life & Works of Surrealist Egyptian Poet Joyce Mansour." *Cairo Scene,* January 14, 2025. https://cairoscene.com/artsandculture/the-life-works-of-surrealist-egyptian-poet-joyce-mansour

Sade, Marquis de. *Justine, or the Misfortunes of Virtue*. Translated by John Phillips. Oxford: Oxford University Press, 2012.

THE PARROT (1956)

In the beginning, when God lived in a hole in the ground, his twin brother slept in the sky, and the universe was shapeless and empty; the last remains of humanity still breathed in the depths muddied by creative thought, in a North African hotel with an ocean view.

The assassin rose, his single needle erect, and grabbed Marie's arm. Bad jokes clouded the sky, and the moist melancholy of the sea filled the room. Marie let her hair out, and the assassin said, "I have a revolting love for you; it makes my solitude a prison—utter hell."

"I understand. There is such misery in my heart; so much night," replied Marie.

But the assassin had moved on. In a single motion, he ripped the woman's grey clothes off with his hand and threw her against the wall, where she stood like a column of blood.

"You're fleshy enough to satisfy me," he grumbled. "I'll hang your sporran over the door, I'll watch the stars fall from your gaping mouth, I will smell the gay and juvenile wiggling of my navel, I will eat of your flesh, and the ferociousness of my sex will be equalled by no other than the fever of my intestinal apparatus."

His voice was drowning, his crystalline tears falling between the woman's breasts; only the parrot, ceremoniously dining at the table in front of the mirror, remained calm.

Marie felt the sweat cling to the hairs along the nape of her neck; her blood pulsed in a motor-like rhythm through her veins. She realized her fear had reached its apex, and, with the room slowly dissipating and the assassin's oilcloth crumpling her uterus, the soft light of her conscience grew wet.

"Everything in women is false, enigmatic," said the assassin. "But there's a word for that mystery: it's wound."

He split the woman's belly in two places with a safety pin: "Here's your truth," he told her with disdain.

In the dark hall of the hotel, the North Africans listened to a potpourri of Slavic sentiments bathing in unsalted cream sauce, accompanied by a side of whinging from a Russian violinist.

The image of God of the Earth flickered before Marie's closed eyes; the assassin discussed the immaculate conception of oxen, and the universe capsized in blood like a giant dead louse. A chair collapsed, and the assassin became angry: "Every man is a potential assassin, but I, the watchful bear, am the one who creates. I will spawn rage's child, and on that day, there will be no end to the massacre."

Marie wasn't listening. Alone in a world illuminated by the phosphorescence of cruelty, she was unable to flee from the torment she condoned, a human bird in wet fur prey to a hunter of her choosing.

The parrot belched. It was a Belgian parrot.

That night, while the sea, agitated by the cold, incandescent moon, rubbed against the pebbles of the beach, Marie opened the window wide, for despair dwelt within her. The secret world of hate, the love of jealous women, the mineral light of intellect—all these were part of her, and her desire for another way of life felt unbearable. The days emerged from the swamp in a straight line, and the assassin moved through the mire of her life with the heavy, blinding speed of a raccoon. "This has to end," she told herself, but the assassin wouldn't kill her, and the old man, Jérémie, watched her day and night.

"So you don't do anything stupid," he said.

In the extended silences, the parrot played the role of a pencil sharpener with Jérémie. They indulged in endless sessions of intercourse before the mirror, then took pleasure in generously ejaculating into a cracked pot. Only the assassin slept. Weary from his day at the slaughterhouse, he slept, carved from the granite of his social superiority. He was king, the aristocrat of strength, and his destitute subjects surrendered to silence while he slept.

Marie shut the window, no longer seeing the blaze of lights from the coffee shops reflected in the water, for the moon was rising, mysterious behind the night's moving membrane.

"Open up!" barked the assassin, eyes still white from sleep, with his hands folded over his chest. "Only the poor get cold feet."

He rose, casually undressed Marie, and poured her between himself and the mattress. The old man touched the parrot delicately; an Arabic tune from the neighbouring room where a Bedouin was dreaming upon the remains of a camel pierced the divide. Marie, sprawling in the great leaf of her vaginal frailty, said, "Kill a rabbit; I'll make a coat." And the assassin sneered.

Weeks and years passed, dragging their old shoes in the room overlooking the harbour, until the day Marie, shaking

Jérémie, who was playing dice with the parrot, said, "That's it. Fight it out. You all disgust me, playing games for a few pennies, breath reeking of cigarettes."

The players stared at her, stunned, and then went back to throwing their dice. "She's crazy," said Jérémie, shaking his head, and the parrot closed one eye.

Marie held her long black locks between her thumb and index finger, twisted them around a fork, and slowly shaved her head and eyebrows. The sun struck the bedroom wall where the woman's gently arched body outlined the plain gilding of her profile.

She tossed her hair in the middle of the table, between the fromage blanc and the newspaper. Rivers of evil began to flow between the furniture.

"Jérémie, you old upright corpse, wipe your mouth!" she screamed at him.

But Jérémie rolled a double six and hid in a corner, saying, "My soul has a long ladder. It goes up and down like a squirrel without catching its breath, only Marie makes it dizzy and it falls, the poor soul, breaking its teeth."

The last rays of sun withered on the mountainside.

"Let us pray," said the parrot, kneeling, and the assassin gently closed the door.

"Get me something to drink, you old goat sorcerer, and you, girl, bring me something to eat," he said, surreptitiously rubbing himself against a corner of the table.

He ate and drank to the point of nausea. Then he dropped his pants and glued Jérémie to the wall with a lot of saliva and Seccotine. He ripped Marie from her reverie, kneaded her open cheeks, around which loitered an old blind fly, and lit the candles while he sang:

"I will plant a phallus
In every bottle of milk
I will slit my wrists
I will rape my mother
I will do it all just to please you
And the filth will flow like honey
On your old appanage
Then, vibrating like a planet,
I will enter your flesh
And the filth will flow like honey
It's cheaper than beer."

Marie didn't move, as if listening to an inspired voice rising from the abyss, and her breasts, erect as hunting dogs, sniffed the wind.

The assassin danced on tiptoe. His head fell now to the right, now to the left, like a withered flower at the end of its stem; his body spun, arms stretched out like a cross, and time, clammy with tension, whirled as well. At the end of a long tunnel of silence, a ticking watch.

"God approaches," said Marie. "Come, God with the long ears."

She spread her legs in front of the assassin's knife. He cut her in the raw flesh of her immense scream, and the woman's shudders echoed in the smallest crevasses of her being. "Finish me off!" spat Marie from the depths of her pain. And the sound of her voice burst the old man's eardrum.

The assassin then turned to Jérémie, who was still stuck to the wall, and tore the rags that covered his greyish legs. "Naked. We must stand naked before death and before God."

With these words, he pulled Jérémie's head toward him and screwed a lit candle into his eye. "You too must see the light!" he screamed.

He lit a second candle and stuck it in the dead woman's ass, saying, "Your poor fly needs a guide."

Then, kneeling next to the icon, he said, with such sadness, "Oh Marie, with your belly coated in membranes, Marie, mother of the world, sister of innocents, I carved a path with my horns through the thicket of your womb, a path to the Heavens. Dethrone those divinities who mock the poor. Avenge mankind, Marie—don't forget mankind!"

The monstrous ticking filled the room, the electric currents making each object incandescent, and thousands of eyes glowed like dimples of light around the prone woman. Jérémie dropped his candle, and God took off, coughing.

"It is finished," said the assassin with satisfaction. "Perhaps we'll have peace now." He rose, turned the dead woman toward the wall, and covered her with a sheet.

"One less face in the rain, yet another unsmiling clod of earth. We are but mud, and this we know, and the worm, that little white sausage, knows this better than any of us."

The parrot poked his head out from a hole in the wall and said, "A word to the wise."

"Word!" said the assassin. And he wiped his mouth because the taste of blood was revolting.

"Would you like some fresh cheese?" shouted the neighbour, hitting the partition.

"Peace!" answered the parrot.

And the assassin smiled.

Sticky as he was, Jérémie threw himself on the bed. Tears filled his eyelids. In death, Marie was able to follow her idea to the depths of the Earth, to the abyss of abysses, embracing the sound wave all the way to the edge of the final membrane.

"The devil follows his master," said the old man, crossing himself. "Deliver us from Your Dog."

He was fed up with all the party games.

JULIUS CAESAR (1955)

They were born together in Sodom to a cow and a grave-digger after two hours of labour washed down with plenty of beer. They lay between the damp and seldom-laundered sheets of the paternal bed and almost immediately regretted the warmth of the uterine embrace. They enjoyed the delicacies of endless renal secretions; the freedom of the navel delighted them. Clinging to the honey-gorged udders of their wet nurse, Julius Caesar, they swore to each other in sweet babbles that they would drink all the blood in the world. They were normal children.

The father leaned his simian head over the battleground where his wife struggled with the twins and the last gasps of her pains, and he left to earn the household bread by the sweat of his brow, pants unzipped, unshaven, surrounded by tears, corpses, and worms for cenotaphs.

It all took place on a mountain as big as France, surrounded by lakes, clouds shaped like heads, and enemy countries. Brave villagers lived there in peace with their goiters and beasts, unconcerned with the future, while they sold the blood of their veins and clocks to mobile hospitals. The sun glazed the lakes; the fields were rich with cows.

Children learned their lessons on balconies flanking smiling precipices. Dressed up like Parisian schoolchildren but with a guttural, mountainous dialect in their buttered-up mouths.

At night, everyone danced to the sounds of the sanitarium, and semen flowed in the streets; of course, everything was set up to attract tourists.

Like every mother who has lovingly sheltered children for nine months beneath her corset, the mother was intent on recovering her figure for the dresses she hoped to don again once her loosened muscles answered the call. She, who had stroked her growing belly, who had shown it to relatives with pride and skillfully concealed it from her lovers. She who had fed the moving tumour with her fat, who had aired it out, masked it, smeared it with rouge on holidays, dunked it in streams to drown the evil eye; she could now only think of how to make it disappear, to the point of starving herself before breakfast.

Unfamiliar with any notion of hygiene, she would have let the twins die of filth and starvation rather than lift a ribboned finger. Fortunately, there was Julius Caesar. The children loved their mother with an enormous, wounded love. They showed their sorrow by baring their gums ferociously every time she approached the cradle. Jealous, she threw slaps left and right to Julius Caesar, who didn't always manage to catch them, and who, saddled with two kids and a goat, had better things to do. The blows that didn't land exhausted on the bed, flew out the window, imagining themselves butterflies enamoured with the sun, lost in the enormous croaking ennui of the afternoon. Life lollygagged on the sandy roads, and, slowly, the peaks melted into the memories of hikers.

The mother, lazy and naked, ambled along the streets, shopping and daydreaming. She enjoyed the futility of her life among the stones with their human faces and the peasants built like rocks. She felt divine, although without admirers, and her movements became symbols before she even drew them. It was a kind of paradise populated with dissolved dreams. She thought of the snails she would sow in the fall, of her husband's mended undergarments that floated around him like wet wings, and of Julius Caesar's smouldering anger.

As for Julius Caesar, she was old and wicked and grew more Black every year, but she had made herself indispensable to the goat, and the mother could not bring herself to fire her despite their frequent run-ins, which regularly knocked her down in the hallways.

Like the twins, the empty windows smiled fiercely when the mother walked by, and the village streets, overshadowed by the green church built by fifteenth-century monks, seemed sadder than usual. The dust no longer kicked up at the passing of dishevelled wagons, and the oxen dropped large cakes of manure with every step. "Summer is over," the mother told herself. "Yet another year hangs beneath my arms." She picked up her purple-rimmed breasts with a large sigh and tied them around her neck; evenings are cool in the mountains.

The mother greeted a neighbour, a cousin, and a cat. "Everyone knows each other," she told herself. "They know the colour of my skin; they know how clumsy my husband is when he comes home drunk, the goat on his back and his socks hardened with snow. The neighbours know that at dawn, enchanted by the moist pleasures of daybreak, I walk the fields, my feet torn by the dew and my mouth bleeding, happy. They know that Julius Caesar wears different coloured garters to hold up the fading flesh of her sixty years.

They know my house." She sighed, and her gaze faded into the duck pond. It's hard to be a goddess amongst peasants.

She wasn't unhappy. Her husband was mostly gone, and this dead-end village satisfied her desire to feel superior. The anger and envy of her neighbours snowed down on her skin, and her thighs broke into a sweat every time a malicious glance grazed them.

The little path, climbing through the brambles and mushrooms toward the cottage perched amongst the pines, carried the mother on its hunched back, and Julius Caesar's white eyes shone in the night, lighting the more difficult passages. "She's going to attract mosquitoes," grumbled the mother. "I won't even wash my feet; dirt faints in the darkness, and I'll sleep better under my blankets of dust, like furniture, happy in the greyness of my faded slumber."

The twins grew up in an atmosphere of unsuppressed loathing. The mother and Julius Caesar would pet each other furiously in corners, searching for little creatures under their aprons. With gritted teeth and hair standing on end, they insulted each other in forgotten languages with cavernous belly voices. Around the cradle were only snapdragons and screams of hatred, and the twins counted their fingers and mewed with fear.

The whole family detested the father for his drunken ways and his tobacco-yellowed moustache that always fell into the soup. They wished him dead, and even the goat bit his hand when he tried to pet it. The mother sought revenge on the father by recruiting random lovers—at the post office, in the streets, or among her husband's green clients. She threw tantrums on nights he needed sleep, terrifying the whole household. She would throw him into the hallway, shivering from the cold, miserable, his hair bristling beneath his nightcap. Unable to sleep on the floor, he spent nights buffeted between the goat's pungent straw and Julius Caesar's no less odoriferous bed. She would finish the poor man off with oddly aggravating caresses that left him completely stunned the next day.

It was a family like any other family, and the twins grew up in the sunshine, full of sap and grand plans. They cut their teeth on the bones of one of the goat's parents, learned to walk alongside ducklings, ate without understanding why, and loved each other more and more fiercely. "We'll have to bathe them soon," the mother told herself.

Women of a certain age go crazy over the smallest things—a mosquito bite on a butt cheek swollen with bitterness, a lover gone cold, or a menopause slow to declare itself.

The mother realized she was crazy when the beige curtains of her room, devoid of all personality until then, got a hard-on. It was quite embarrassing, especially at night when she was naked before her open window, massaging her belly under the approving gazes of her neighbours. "I should have surgery," she told herself. And she shredded the curtains, stiff with pleasure, using Julius Caesar's scissors.

Things worsened when the twins started attending the local school. The mother began crawling on all fours, decorated with a single crow feather between her butt cheeks and singing old Viennese waltzes in a strong bass voice. She was convinced that the walls were accompanying her and that her husband was jealous of the tenor, in this instance, Julius Caesar. She became violent when her mother-in-law came for tea, imagining her husband planting corpses in the kitchen, and her screams were abominable to hear. "The neighbours will talk," the father told himself. "She needs to be calmed down."

So, on a night of the full moon, they set off together—rusty chains around their necks and years of deprivation in their hearts—into the mountain, behind the chalet, among the pines with trembling tops and the grey stones—nature's smiling wisdom teeth. There he forced his wife to her knees, gripping her firmly by her hair, and brutally forcing her legs open while plunging his tongue into her navel, bending her backward until her head touched the ground. He spent a long time cleaning his wife's body of its familiar demons. Finally, moved by the limp nakedness of his submissive wife, he lay her down on the grass grazed by the moon—tongue lolling, seemingly asleep—and took her without even undressing. Lying on her, he dug his teeth into her stretched and gasping neck and sucked. He scraped her, covered her body with earth, and spit fresh bile into her eyes. He fondled her flesh feverishly and then, his rage subsiding, crossed himself saying, "Pray that it not be twins again."

The mother felt no pain. She languished on the ground, her legs bowed, flooded with dew, licked by the night's stray dogs, her breasts whispering to each other, her head emptying slowly between the father's greedy gums.

The man stood up, spit out a tooth, and split the mother's breasts with his thumbs up. "Let's go home," he said. "My feet hurt."

JULIUS CAESAR'S STORY

"My head died with him. I'm nothing more than a cone-shaped pile with hands extraordinarily alive, which leave every morning for the factory to earn a living. For we must go on living, even without a head. I left my last baby tooth in my husband's mouth—he died of financial atrophy—and I prepared for the funeral.

"I borrowed a black dress, pleated with a thousand memories, too wide at the hips, too narrow at the chest, and buried my friend on the day of our engagement.

"The women, bearers of wind, sipped coffee without seeing each other, without batting an eyelash, without tears, around the cadaver laid out in the parlour between the broken piano tail and the ornamental Chinese vases, screaming in agony. His gleaming chrome coffin was the pride of his family, and the flowers that had been brought out of the closet for the occasion were as stiff as the cadaver they covered. A strong odour of mothballs emanated from the coffin; my mother thought it was on account of the flowers.

"I stood beside him, as I had stood by his bed at the hospital, my head filled with debauchery, my hands sweaty. From time to time, I ironed his body, which had a tendency to swell, with a heavy electric iron. 'It's the heat,' my mother would say."

His mother woke up when the men came to take him. She was sleeping in a child's chair at the end of the room, and her patched dress was adorned with reddish stains at the knees, no doubt cat urine. She served tea to these men without schedules, who, bowler hats in hand, scratched themselves in silence. She then led the wailing women with tarred hair to the cemetery, to the waiting hole. "This is how I buried my friend," sighed Julius Caesar. And she undid her corset.

The twins left without kissing their nurse. They knew she was friendless; her life had begun at their birth. It was clear that before that date, she had lived without shelter, purpose, joy, or memory. A servant.

Julius Caesar was born a farmer, her head heavy with hay. But the proximity of cows and the dawn awakenings had opened her eyes to God and His consequences. It must have slipped from her full mouth to furnish her night shifts. She sat on her immense derrière in the middle of the living room, and with her finger pointed toward the ceiling, perforated by the smoke of her cigar, she initiated the twins to the joys of country life. The lessons took the shape of monologues, occasionally interrupted by resounding burps from the goat and the muffled applause of the rain against the windows. "If God is dead, everything is dead, and we are nothing but a clump of droppings still warm from the divine breath."

"Steal only the money that your father earns; it's been stolen on your behalf. By stealing it, you erase his guilt. Don't die in front of your mother; the sight of dead babies doesn't frighten mothers. Even after being torn apart, mothers end up feeding off the blood that is yours.

"Be chaste like the powerful, but not necessarily abstinent. The old are abstinent without being chaste, and their crutches are witness to the shame of their solitude. Wash your hands before going to bed, or your dreams will smell like your days."

She would tell the children even more, thumbs in their mouths, and their dolls' eyes remained wide open for a long time.

The twins quickly learned the usefulness of blasphemy. It was their wine, the proof of their immense love for Him, their cruelest game. The mother, always dressing for inclement weather, left the children in the hands of the priest for any religious teachings, and, apart from uttering a few curse words, never spoke of Him.

The priest was fat, bald, and sleepy. The climb to the cottage tired him; he visited as infrequently as possible. The children's visits to the rectory, accompanied by Julius Caesar, were purely social in nature, since the wet nurse was too modest to allow for any serious conversation in her presence. That's how, without anyone's help, the twins built cathedrals in their heads and decorated them with a thousand baroque superstitions. As they grew older, the rituals they invented became more complicated and left their practitioners, clothed with scraps of flesh and leftover food, increasingly dissatisfied.

In the beginning, Julius Caesar was God. A comforting and hassle-free God until the day she fell ill and her fear, in the doctor's presence, tore the veil of her divinity.

Reeling from this first disappointment, the children

took several days before selecting a new place for their God. The doctor seemed a good fit, but he wore glasses, which automatically disqualified him. The portrait of the grandfather, hanging in the darkest corner of the living room, drew their attention. Humbly, they adored him.

Crouching on the floor, their blind dolls on their knees, they contemplated the face of their God and insulted him at will until the moment when it seemed that God, impatient and roused from his dust, moved. Their most unanswerable prayers were then fulfilled, and calm returned to the dolls' beds.

Unfortunately, God was unable to protect himself from the hands of the father, who, armed with a kitchen knife, began to scrape the portrait in the hope of discovering a masterpiece. The children awaited a miracle, but the god limply let it happen, immobile and smiling. The canvas gave way under the father's reckless knife. The children, disgusted by this eviscerated god, who suffered without even altering his smile, breakfasted in silence, without appetite. "We will bury our dolls this afternoon," they told Julius Caesar, who knitted in her usual emptiness. They set off in search of a god.

After burying their toys near the pond where the sun sets without troubling the bronze waters, they plucked the canary. Then, with every bit of their childish strength, they called upon God by eating, pissing, and even sleeping in the silence of their dreams, punctuated with uncoordinated erotic movements and hiccups resulting from digestive upsets. But God made himself very small, and their patience shrank a little more each year.

One night, watching for His arrival through the window, with little frozen feet, liquid chemises running over round bums, it seemed to them that the moment was right for a sign that would end their anguished nights. But the stars, as always, shone idiotically, the wind continued to blow without obstacles, and the snow fell on the world with indifference. "He'll never come in the snow," thought the children. Inconsolable, they fell asleep mouth to mouth.

After many years of fresh air and snow, exercise finally chased God from their heads, and sex, heavy with complexes, hardened their hearts. It was the beginning of adolescence, and their skin rose in protest, bursting into hot pimples under Julius Caesar's nose. "We'll have to pop them," the mother said to herself.

Lucie, the daughter of the lumberjack who killed men when he had time, burst brilliantly into the twins' lives. She was sitting quietly in the woods behind her father's cottage, cleaning her nails with a fork, waiting, like every woman whose breasts cluck under their corsets, for a man. She was beautiful, with red hair, waxed legs glistening in the sunshine, and her never-ending hands.

The twins were hunting. Their quarrelsome voices broke the icy silence of the morning, and the sound of their boots on the ground hardened by the night broke the hearts of the animals who slept in their path. They stopped in front of the virgin Lucie, and the morning star faded without a sigh. The twins, used to the perpetually pregnant village girls with their goiters hanging down to their chests, were immediately seduced. The virgin lifted a finger with a detached air and pointed the way to the cottage.

"Who are you?" exclaimed the twins, sexes in disarray.

"Lucie," said the virgin with a heavy feminine neigh.

The least pimply twin moved closer and said foolishly, "You are so beautiful, you must taste of milk."

"I am the only being in all of these ultra-civilized mountains who cannot read," she answered with indifference.

"Yes, but you are so beautiful, and we are rude and ugly like calves," said one of the twins, staring at his mud-crusted boots.

"And those who are not ugly are old," said the other.

"You must kill to be beautiful, kill with your eyes closed, kill with violence, kill, kill, kill. We kill all the time at my father's. I will teach you if you like," said the virgin. And her shining eyes seemed filled with little waves.

The twins understood that God was feminine; their heads spun on their shoulders like weathervanes. "Let's see each other often," said the virgin; her chest was jiggling under her tunic. "I am often bored."

But the twins, jealous of one another for the first time in their lives, kept their mouths shut, each waiting for the other to answer. "You're dumb," said the virgin, picking up her little white uterus, and she left, crumpling it between her fingers, shaking with her bird laugh.

The twins tore their eyes painfully from her haunches and swore to return the next day at the latest. Julius Caesar tried to calm them with buttered bread, but her efforts were in vain, and she left. "The virgin Lucie," she said, "lives with a madman who cuts down men and trees all day long; it's unhealthy. You will bring death to the house; death is contagious, and I am old. I am old." But the twins were not superstitious. They knew that death was a marvellous thing when you were done with living, and they continued to see Lucie every day.

Julius Caesar had not left the attic window since dawn. She stood, leaning on her calloused elbows, nose eaten by the cold, feet bloated with blood, scanning the countryside with her gaze. "She must be ill," the mother told herself, and she went up to the attic.

"It's the end of the world," said Julius Caesar, nodding her head. "Look." She made room for the mother, who saw nothing exceptional. The sky hung in heavy curtains, occasionally illuminated by smiles of light; the mountains slept in the same uncomfortable positions, and the grass had not changed colour.

"It's the end of the world," repeated Julius Caesar stubbornly. "You don't have to believe me. You'll see, you'll see." And without any further explanation, she went downstairs to pack her bundle.

"More like the end of the month," answered the mother vulgarly, because she knew Julius Caesar's follies. "Calm, she needs some calm," she said, and went to inspect the latrines.

The next day, one hour after rising from the table, while the father was drunk and dripping with sauce and the mother was spilling out of her chair, corset unbuttoned to breathe more easily, Julius Caesar announced for the third time, "The world is ending today," opening the door to the garden in a gesture à la Sarah Bernhardt. The father and a twin followed her while she marched with a decided step toward the edge of the woods to contemplate the much-anticipated debacle. They caught up to her among the forest's first trees, then waited for a sign, holding their breaths. But nothing moved. No tree had fallen; no lightning tore the sky. Everything was calm, strangely normal. Somewhat disappointed, they prepared to scold Julius Caesar for her idiocy when they both noticed that the silence had an unsettling quality and there was nothing left alive in the woods. "Strange," said the father. "Let's go back."

At the cottage, everything was in its usual place, and the village in the distance seemed as sleepy as usual. "We musn't try to understand everything," said the father. "It's time for rest." And he threw himself on his bed, satisfied with his explanation.

But Julius Caesar, head between her knees, listened expectantly to the silence of the countryside, to the silence of the birds, and to the silence of the shadow lurking under the trees like a frigid, frightened beast. She sang to quiet her fear, swaying her steel curls. "It's the end of my pain, Lord, the End. Protect us from the fear to come; it is the moment to repent everything. Protect us, Lord; we are crowned in thorns, and the grave is open in the depths of our misery." And it began to rain, and Julius Caesar understood that God hadn't had time to listen.

It rained for months. The rivers, gorged with villages and earth, ran toward the plain, leaving behind them seas of fresh water and lamentations punctuated by telegraph poles.

In the beginning, the mayor of the village said, "It's good

for the ducks, very good, very good," rubbing his hands jovially. Then he said, "It will stop at Easter." And then he said nothing at all; everyone had become used to it. But Julius Caesar knew it was the end of the world. She stayed quiet.

Nights of rain, days of rain. Rain in houses beating against the walls; rain like a fountain, bursting nature's bowels; rain, always rain, in heads, in singing buckets, in mouths, in sleepers' genitals, in the dark alcoves of churches; rain everywhere. And the wound came out of hiding, the wound that the devil carries on his flank that is called "orgasm." And God spat out the monotonous rain, the rain weary of raining, the hysterical rain trying to break everything, the rain snivelling over sunless sunsets, the rain, while the village, bogged down in the open wound, rotated according to a fixed axis flooded by the glassy reflections of rain. And the sky, like a breast of luscious suffering, screamed.

The twins, dripping with happiness, visited the virgin Lucie every day. She always greeted them the same way: "You again? What exactly do you want?" And she would rise from the moss, more naked than in the summer, shivering in a tawny fox coat that opened at the slightest movement, uncovering her greenish body while her coiled hair flamed. The twins loved her with all the fever of adolescence. They loved watching her body dissolve in the pond's dead waters; they loved to ride her horseback like a victim and gallop until the horse dropped with exhaustion; they loved to find her motionless as a beast, her body stained with sadness, her face passive under her fiery hair, attentive to the sounds of Hell. They learned to caress her.

Her father, the lumberjack, lived his own life. He cut down trees faster than they could grow; he littered the forest with useless, uncut corpses. He felled men when he felt like it, and the ones he killed, he chopped up and buried in a hidden location known only to him. He was a lumberjack and he loved his work. When the rain made the fallen trees rot, he considered burying them, but the morbid indolence of putrefaction tied even the lumberjack's hands. Folded in two, he slept instead of toiling.

The rain continued to fall, and the mayor sighed, "Who knows if it's raining in the next village?" But no one had the strength to go see. The graves were melting under the incessant rain; coffins grimaced between tombstones. "Might be better to bury them again before they start walking around," he declared. But the gravedigger was sleeping up there, in the cottage, and no one could be bothered to wake him. The newspapers were no longer being delivered, the radio had gone silent, the mute telephone snored without answering, and the wind slept upright on the highest peak, shrouded in fog. The village, weary of living, was preparing to drown.

By Pentecost it was still raining, and the water rose in the valley. The countryfolk slept, their tasks unfinished, barely eating, stifled by the monotony of their long slumber.

The greatest tragedy was that of the cows.

They roamed among the houses, begging in low voices for the shuttered-in sleepers to relieve their udders, which dragged between their legs, dribbling sanguineous milk. Others, mad from the pain, rolled on the ground, trying to milk themselves, or else ran after imaginary hands that danced like bats in moonbeams. The farmers, awakened for a few moments, shook their heads and said, "It's a sign of the times, chatty women, war, cows thinking they're race-horses. What will become of us?" And they would fall asleep again, opened-mouthed, stunned by the rain.

The calves, gorged with milk, could no longer move and finally burst, splashing the moist fields with finely sliced vitello tonnato. As their udders filled, they rooted themselves in the earth, and the now anchored cows ceased their bellowing, delighted to let themselves be milked by the worms. "They look like mushrooms," a farmer observed while inspecting the fields between slumbers, one eye swollen with sleep.

In the cottage, Julius Caesar knit in her sleep. The mother, happy in her obscenity, also slept, with her feverish, swollen belly escaping her corset. The father slept. The twins stroked the barbed breasts of the virgin Lucie, and the goat chewed on the canary.

Lucie felt the need to be caressed; her body stiffened when a hand grazed it, and her feet, shaking with giggles, danced. As a child, she had rubbed herself against trees with protruding branches and rolled in the moss, or, legs spread and bristling with happiness, she had played secretive games with her dolls. The twins indulged in her tamed animal games with wild desires. "What peace there is in your eyes, dearest Julius Caesar, now that they are closed," said one twin as he pierced the maid's bodice with his finger. Then Lucie took the Black woman's abundant breasts between her lips, and all three ate of her flesh. When the feast was finished, Lucie closed the open lips of the wound, and the twins threw themselves on the couch where the canary was dying, forgetful of everything except their bodies and Lucie's unsatisfied eyes.

A thick drizzle fell on the mountains. The father interrupted his sleep with troublesome moments of terrifying lucidity. The village before his eyes was drowning, house by house; the villagers, drunkenly sprawled on their beds, were dying while the water rose in the valley with satisfying gurgles. "In one week, we'll have wet feet," he told Julius Caesar, who was sleeping, her bottom discoloured from the cold.

The dialogue was dead before it began, and the father chewed on his solitude with rancour. He tried to wake his wife for a chat. At first, he patted her cheeks, saying, "Hey, little mother; hey, little flower," but hit with impotence from the limpness of her reactions, he began to beat her with the iron.

As though a bomb had exploded in his skull, his brain seemed to flutter, like a bird held captive for too long, now free and drunk. He struck, scratched, poked, laughed. He resented the mocking sexes pinned to the wall and destroyed their ability to move by biting the testicles hidden beneath the foliage. The mother, a pile of worked-over meat devoid of any personality, moaned on the ground, steaming with pain. Julius Caesar rolled over in her bed and went back to sleep. A twist of luck brought the lumberjack, in search of food, to the cottage door, where he remained awhile, contemplating the carnage, somewhat intimidated. Then he tore off the mother's head with a single bite and went to find something to eat. The mother, dead in her printed dress, let her head roll under the table, and her legs took flight for one last time before rooting themselves in the stillness of Hell. Dead, she was so naked and so deliciously obscene that the father, overcome with remorse, began to miss her.

What's most incredible about these types of hallucinations is that their essence is borrowed from reality. The lumberjack, his belly full of cheese and honey, thought he recognized his own head under the table, bleeding meaty bubbles and juicy with flies. He brought his big face as close as he could to the mask, which contracted and seemed to snicker. The lumberjack opened his mouth, chalky with cheese, and howled; the last convulsions of the decapitated mother coincided with his desperate screaming and mad escape. Nostrils plugged with blood, his brain burning with horror, he threw himself into the abyss.

Meanwhile, the father, flattened against the floor, was kissing the petrified features of the woman he had married.

"She was a good housekeeper," he said, his mouth smeared with his victim's blood. He blubbered pityingly. Alone with his beloved, alone with his pathetic desires to deepen his own suffering, he brought the truest expression of his impulses to the slaughterhouse and cut up the featureless mask instead of framing it. Sleep began to overcome him. He sat at the table in the company of the corpse and placed his leaden head amongst the wreckage of the last family supper. From then on, absence and vastness would be this man's wife. She was everywhere. Immobile as ecstasy, the arabesques of her modesty protected the nakedness of the pubis (that pubis hollowed by a thousand repetitive pleasures, also dead), temptress without any power of betrayal, naked, irrevocably naked, his thing. She was the very essence of the ether; she had lent her scent to the earth, and he entered completely, in silence, all obstacles abolished, as he dissolved in the pale seed that finally erased nakedness. "I will eat the spider of her enormous desire, I will drink menstrual blood from the source of ignominy, and her death will be consumed," he said, knowing he, too, was damned.

The damned, blinded, contemplate the world from their hollow sockets, their mouths filled with the entrails of their hallucinations and their prison doors maybe forever locked by the monstruous shudder of exhaustion. Their excuse is always the same: unrequited love. And their tears are acid with truth.

The father slept, woke up, and, after wiggling momentarily, scratched under his arm, rubbed his eyes, cleared his throat, and tried to speak, but not a word could escape his mouth. There was something lost in this new man's gaze, uncertain of his weight. "Turning over would be delightful," he thought as he collapsed and fell asleep again.

Julius Caesar removed the corpse, cleaned the floor where the rats were playing, and went up to the attic. There, without interrupting the twins' and the virgin's subtle games—they were tattooing thighs and the bushy swell of the belly—she announced the mother's death and the lumberjack's suicide. "My father has always loved the outdoors," said Lucie. "There's no need to bury him; he'll sort himself out." And she offered her tumultuous mouth to the twins' claws.

The father came to see Julius Caesar and said in an engaging tone, "I threw off some ballast. Tomorrow I'll build a raft."

"Start at dawn," answered the maid to show she wasn't afraid. "And now nothing is stopping you from taking a nap if your heart so desires. You look terrible."

"My gut hurts," growled the father, and he showed the pale outlines of his belly button.

"Emotion is an empty stomach," diagnosed Julius Caesar. "Sleep."

And the rain drowned the goat's lamentations.

Wearing a tiny, white woollen cap, the father worked on the raft. Days passed. And nights. Fruitful nights of murder and rape where he lost everything, even the buttons of his shirt and his few remaining hairs. It was a true honeymoon—he had never loved his wife more. At night, he had noticed the presence of different-sized breasts, swollen with pride, floating seemingly aimlessly around his bed. But when he awoke looking for them, still gripped by the icy burn of his dreams, they had disappeared. Surely they had deflated and fallen in a corner of the room and were hiding in the chaos of used underwear and fish bones. The rain fell, heavy and sticky, and the father worked without trying to understand the delight of his imaginings, not in the least bit burnt by his damnation. "He thinks he's Noah," laughed the twins. "Don't forget the urinal; it's essential on a raft." And they fell into fits of laughter that made the mountains tremble. Lucie, with her gamey freshness, called to them. Dressed in flattering quotations, her tongue loaded with honey, she called them, and the twins felt the velvety tingling ripen in their groin, flourish in their bellies like fireworks. They followed the maiden in her peregrinations through the windswept woods. They made her moan, lying at their feet, adorned with a charm of a stag's masculine stump, breasts hardened with determination. "I reign over these animals," thought Lucie, and she bit deeply into earth saturated with sadness, proud of her martyrdom.

Julius Caesar tended to the goat. "Life is quite sad when it's raining," she thought. And the rain fell, meowing on the roof of the cottage over the remains of a cat.

The raft, made of foam, mucus, and refuse, was finally ready. With the father's work done and the water still a few feet from the cottage, he found himself idle and got drunk. And during his final drinking binge, he ruminated. He thought about the warm vital organs of the goat in his fingers, and he ate them. He thought about his two sons, always searching for the great mystery hidden beneath women's skirts. He knew that even in death, this furious activity would continue relentlessly, because the twins were in love with sex, and their corpses' vocations would be the same, with the ground as their womb and the other dead as accomplices. He thought of the horses floating in the valley, between half-swallowed chimneys and tufts of foliage. He thought of the rain, of the red curtains of New York brothels, and of the dead who were calling him in the wind that rose up from the valley. He was sad. He remembered with pain his wife who was already dissolved into the grey alcohol irrigating his brain. "She could piss all the way to the ceiling, lying on her back," he said through gritted teeth, and he ripped out the weeds cluttering the fly of his pants. He remembered with ease the Chinese woman who, under her kimono, smack against her body, hid a hedgehog crackling with electricity that had to be pet while discussing the weather before he could grab her. How intoxicating she was, that prickly moss, spongy and musical, and the father choked at the memory. He reprimanded his lowing groin, mouth open like a calf, and sat down. It was at this moment that a very rare physiological interlude amongst peasants occurred. The father began to menstruate. The cognac burned his throat and made his face, with its ears spread wide, shine, while he menstruated from all of his pores and orifices. He barked furiously, broke himself in half, and spread his entrails on the floor. He looked with astonishment at the smoking, squirming eels and ripped them from his insides without even knowing they existed. He crushed them with his foot, and the blood spurted. His heat lingered long into the night, and his drunkenness morphed into a clot of mucus that dripped on his old, bewildered face unnoticed. "Blow your nose!" screamed Julius Caesar, her eyes bulging with disgust. "It's raining enough without you adding to it!" But the father knew it wasn't just blood and saliva he was losing; it was his most intimate time of the month. He grew very afraid of the future.

Julius Caesar woke one morning with a solid lump of worry stuck to the walls of her pubis. She understood that it was serious; the cause of her fear was twofold: the twins.

She thought of their noisy childhood amongst the goat droppings and the wildflowers that grew between the kitchen tiles. She remembered the crumpled faces of their toys, their games in the fields, and their soft animal naps with moist mouths, rich with stores of smiles. She sighed: "They've grown up without my even noticing, those rascals!" And the inevitability of her solitude hardened the ball of worry even more. She thought about the school, now more drowned than spaghetti in soup, where she had left them every morning with eyes full of tears and hands grasping at her shopping basket. Now they were enormous, two fellows, faces blue with beards and steady voices. Taller than the father who seemed to shrink a little in size every year, much taller than her...

Julius Caesar was proud of these twins, almost beautiful under their bushy hair, but she knew she was useless in their eyes: from God to domestic. It was rough. They no longer listened to her and laughed at the words of an illiterate old Black woman, pinching her large cheeks and saying, "Go on, Julius Caesar, the goat's calling."

With adolescence came a visual curiosity previously unknown to Julius Caesar's world—cows, mountains, forests, and even the market. It came from a desire to understand the machinations of secrecy. The twins' conversation had become opaque, solid, with a technical taste, and their faces teemed with maggots. The thirst to see with the naked eye, to touch, with the fingertips, the sacred place, trembling, still hairless and hidden under skirts that smelled of hay, consumed them. And the pleasure of discussing and endlessly debating the subject was fascinating. Nothing else interested them, especially not Julius Caesar's redundant tales. They had become secretive—their games stopped as soon as Julius Caesar approached; their stern faces sparkled with hate at the intruder's slightest blunder. Later, they would meet Lucie, the little mad girl of the woods, and Julius Caesar would once again feel dethroned forever. Night fell softly under the rain, and Julius Caesar was sad. All day, she had thought about the twins and did not see how she could regain her place in their lives nor how she could be rid of her rival. She wanted to bring the twins back under her power, to feel their heads labouring against her chest; she wanted them to drop that fixed gaze of men mad about themselves, and her old mouth mumbled magical words in vain. "I'm going around in circles," she told herself, and then she made a decision she would regret for the rest of her life.

The next day, she left for the mountains in search of the snow god, who, in the guise of a giant ape, had lived since the dawn of time off the human flesh carried to him by the wind. She walked for two days and three nights without rest, and her swollen soul swung on the end of its stem. Then God ceased breathing, and Julius Caesar sat under a rock overlooking the valley. Her red flannel dress stained the snow, and in the distance, blackish peaks dirtied the pure sky. "I walk amongst men as though fragments of the future, powerless against everything that has been done. My will cannot act on the past. To free myself from Lucie, I must act alone. Only then will my invisible walls of solitude crumble." Thus, she reasoned with an anger equal to her desire for domination. Clouds heavy with snow wandered the summits, and Julius Caesar's chest leapt with annoyance. She knew that the great ape would appear but felt her impatience would drive her mad. She promised herself a thousand tempting delights for when, after her revenge, the twins would return to her, small as dwarves and so tender. She harvested her disgust as though it was the only truth, and it stuck to her lips like an oyster. She was expecting a god and was careful not to spit in the wind of vengeance. She waited.

Suddenly, the ape was there. Enormous, he dominated Julius Caesar; the beauty of his sex illuminated her gaze. She closed her legs, yellowed with cold, and her brain fluttered into the unlimited diameters of ecstasy. Her crime burst inside her head like a flower. The monster approached hesitantly, and his breath penetrated her to her deepest terror. She wanted to let herself be taken by this god, who was unaware of his beauty, overcome by this impulse that hardened the very roots of her sex. She struggled, standing in the wind, against the gentleness of her imagination, and won. She threw the shirt, saturated with urine, stiff with sweat and femininity, stolen from Lucie, in the giant's face and ran. The ape sat. He liked the virgin's scent; he smelled her shirt, sucked it, ate it, and, drunk with desire, rolled in the snow, brandishing his sex like a shrub still rigid from winter.

Julius Caesar rolled on her short legs all the way back to the cottage. She seemed to bounce from star to star. The ball of worry had vanished like smoke, and she prepared to savour her vengeance. "The god will deliver me from Lucie. He will come for her, mad with love, drunk with curiosity, and my silence will be the last word that the twins will hear," she told herself. Sadly, the wind answered: "Yes, yes."

Julius Caesar began to run again without meeting a single soul, not even her own; she was alone in the secret silence of multicoloured nightmares.

At the cottage, she found lust swirling, caressing like a rowboat when it touches land, miserable with beauty. The twins' skin swords crossed each other like snakes; their loosened tongues hung around their waists. Lucie, shredded by the lightning of her ecstasy, whinnied. Julius Caesar, consumed with jealousy, faced her defeat. "Wait, my children, the god will deliver me!" she said full of rage, scattering her spittle over the ground. Lucie, on her knees, offered her golden honey. Julius Caesar looked at her with more secrets than pain, and the twins planted their sexes in the darkest of chasms where laughter and fog embrace, where return can only be done walking backward, and where the accumulated ice of desire loses its youth.

The ape showed his face in each of the windows, howled his call into the chimney, and broke down the door. Like the delicious wind dances on the lids of a quiet mother, peace danced in the heart of Julius Caesar. The twins interrupted their rhythm of death; bony in their nakedness, their skin crawling and itching, while flinching, they were afraid.

The god, sick with clotted blood, snatched Lucie from the ground and left.

Without a word, Julius Caesar cleaned the cottage, and the wind swept the snow after the god's departure. Oblivious to everything except their interrupted song, the twins fell into each other's arms and killed the emptiness in the artificial mouth of their imagination by whispering of the virgin's servile belly until their bristling seminal mess was tamed. Julius Caesar ventured into the rain to catch a rabbit with a net. She found the past within arm's reach; her eyes shone like marbles.

After two days of ennui, the twins looked at each other in horror, and their colossal egos bellowed.

Julius Caesar was raking the snow at the cottage door. The father, sitting on the raft, awaited the flood. The goat, clammy with milk, considered suicide, and the mountain air moistened the bushes. It was just another day of rain, but the twins blindly exited the cottage without closing the door and departed. Julius Caesar understood she would never see them again. Barefooted, like children, they set off to find blood, and the pines scattered across the mountainsides like crosses along their path.

And yet, for a long time, Julius Caesar waited. Leaning on her shovel, her soul struggled at the peak of a spring to return to her body, her softened mouth shitting. After an eternity of humiliation, she returned to the cottage, her throat raw from wild sobs. The world seemed to throw off its crutches to fall harder.

During the night, the water swallowed yet another mouthful of land. Without leaving the raft, the father announced to Julius Caesar, "Tomorrow, we leave."

The next day, Julius Caesar, the father, and the goat realized it was indeed time to leave the cottage. The water, only one foot from the door, was still rising. "Since the mother's death, I've only been a shadow," said the father. "I've settled on every surface without experiencing pain; I'm tired of being swung by the wind, tired of tracing my name everywhere she set foot. I will die; I will die as I would have liked to have lived: in a tailcoat." With that, the father zipped his swollen fly from which hung a greedy ox tongue and went to get his suit. Julius Caesar said nothing. The goat still thought of killing herself.

The water, without catching its breath, took the final step toward the cottage. Julius Caesar, without speaking to the hesitant goat, without taking the slightest provision or piece of clothing, sat heavily on the raft. And as a too-rich sun set, Julius Caesar embarked on the chaotic waters, naked except for her hair, still panting with blood, stripped of the future on her shell. The folds of her flesh emptied of parasites, separated from God's undulating belly by just a few planks. And God, liquid of the world's putrefaction, strangled by the endless hiccups of the dying, popped the last mountains with his lost fingers. Lying on her back, soaked to the bone by long, wrenching squirts shooting from the base of the spine, her legs wide, she howled, jet upon jet, her orgasm to the night. And just before the final decomposition, when the last peel of her belly fell, ants came out of the waves of her wound and spread over the raft. They were looking to the horizon for the promised land, but the filth of the negative flood was spreading everywhere, monstrous and inert, an indivisible oneness. And so, Julius Caesar's sex, finally satiated, smiled foolishly at the sky. Her impatient soul yawned.

FLOATING ISLANDS (1973)

Let's review. Torn from a deep sleep by sheer will and a loud scream from my most vicious entrails, I find myself on the shores of lac Léman, in the shallow waters of a waking dream. I cover my left shoulder, protecting it from a draft smelling of laundry and the menacing evil eye of the officer on duty. The dream continues uninterrupted: the same message but a different setting. I'm on a motorboat in Nice. I jump on the dock to make a telephone call, the boat drifts away, the dock sucks in its stomach, and my foot slips... I land elsewhere. I know that when I wake, I run the risk of not finding the real path, having mixed it up in the twilight with the one that is imagined, and which is often much more colourful, more insistent than its reflection. I take a risk. I run dishevelled in the streets of Nice, preceded by a double consonant. "It's not necessary for a lengthened consonant to be doubled," screams a man half running me over with an old American car. And then he says, "It's you! Where are you running to like this?" I recognize Charles G. and as I wonder if it would be possible to do one last back and forth movement on the rustic ride of solitary pleasure without reaching orgasm, I answer out of breath: "I must find the post office, a telephone. I must catch a plane. My father is dying in Geneva." Nevertheless, I think about Charles G.: his great intelligence, his extreme pallor. I remember our calm conversations two years ago on the overcrowded beach of Beauvallon; isolated from the crowd by the flamboyant circle of a toothless parasol, I was half naked, he was fully dressed. I heard screams, barks, and on top of it all, the sour voice of Paul Géraldy[1] scattering his trinkets on the hot sand for three or four pretentious old bags and their dwarf poodles. "Strange," says Charles G., nonchalantly gliding in long, silent lurches toward Antibes, "I was in the same situation as you last year, in this very spot."

The paths, real and imagined, converge. In both cases, I find myself in Geneva.

I am sitting next to the lake on a bench in the sunshine. I examine the two pocketbooks bought at the airport in Nice: *La curée*[2] by Zola and *Le monde désert*[3] by Pierre Jean Jouve. I look at the lake with portrait-like eyes, and I put *La curée* in my suitcase. I dive into the *Le monde désert*: "When the son of a pastor, Isaac de Todi, emerged from his chronic state of reverie to notice that the exterior world, his father's 'country place' in Geneva, was coloured in one fashion or another

1 Paul Géraldy (1885-1983): French poet and dramaturg, author of two collections, *Les Petites Âmes* (1908) and *Toi et moi* (1912).

2 *La curée* by Émile Zola was serialized between 1871–1872 and published in book form in 1872. The second volume in Zola's twenty volume Les Rougon-Macquart series, it centres on financial corruption throughout the Second French Empire. Two more recent English translations of the work, titled *The Kill*, were published by Brian Nelson (2005) and Arthur Goldhammer (2004).

3 Published in 1927 by French author Pierre Jean Jouve, this erotic, psychological novel is set in early twentieth-century Switzerland. It was translated into English as *The Desert World* by American author and translator Lydia Davis in 1996.

by rain or by fair weather, depending on the season and the day, and above all on the unpredictable character of his own soul..." Then, later, the first page: "This was the shore of the lake, pebbly and white."[4]

Does the trajectory of dreams follow the runway for take-off?[5] Pocket dreams. I continue my reading, thus immersing myself in Genevan life in this way. *Le monde désert* is a strange book in which memories overtake present emotions and the clicking sounds of the author's jaw interrupts the text at the worst possible moments. I am constantly losing the thread of the story. I bring myself back by jumping, feet together, as though I want to crush the fragments of my own story. On page ninety-five, my address is transcribed in full letters: "I am on the Quai des Bergues."[6] I have a strong sense that I'm living by proxy, breathing through the pores of the book, having surrendered my powers to "another I," who is also in the snow, in the unlived and outdated. It's not unpleasant. Rather, it's less tiring than the heavy petting of the previous dream. I read Chapter XIII, "Baladine's Story":

"I have to go back to the earliest period of my relationship with Jacques de Todi.

We were living in Geneva. In the new neighbourhood that has been built down there on the edge of the Arve. You know it? The rue des Aubépines isn't a real street, more of a road along which they constructed four or five houses with many stories, and we were in one of them; it goes from rue de Carouge, which is vulgar and working class, to a no-

4 Jouve, Pierre Jean, *The Desert World,* trans. Lydia Davis. (Evanston: Marlboro Press, 1996), 3.

5 Breton, André (ed.), *Trajectoire du rêve: Documents Recueillis.* (Paris: Guy Lévis Mano, 1938).

6 Jouve, *The Desert World,* 63.

man's-land near the Cantonal Hospital. We lived in one of the new houses, on the fifth floor. It was March 1911.

We had found each other again in Lausanne. There's no point in recounting how, it's too complicated. I couldn't live without him any longer, and I probably drew him to me with the force of my thoughts..."[7]

I'll go see that hospital. My father must be there.

I continue my walk in pursuit of Baladine and her lover, Jacques de Todi. "Todi" like everyone?

I cross bridges, streets, hills, walking at the moderate pace of a Swiss pedestrian, burping emphatically, in keeping with the local custom, and spelling out the letters of several alphabets in the hope of i) Not falling over the faintly outlined streetcar tracks while falling asleep; ii) Not falling asleep on the faintly outlined streetcar tomb when I see it; and iii) Not seeing the faint outline of the tomb while falling asleep on the streetcar, etc.

Thus, for the time being I live via the dictation of the author of *Le monde désert*. I follow his plan along dozens of beaches without punctuation or umbrella pines. I experience cases of awakening at the scheduled time. I could find purpose to my peregrinations, but with the increase in the number of signs in the cow pen and the presence of the paternal law through the Word... it's better to stay quiet. Carry on. Everyone must protect their delusion from the intrusion of the pun. Besides, Zola brings to mind the Zohar.[8] I must admit that the fact that my father is agonizing in room 666 of the Cantonal Hospital has nothing to do with my taste in reading.

7 Jouve, *The Desert World*, 49.

8 The Zohar (meaning "Splendour" or "Radiance") is the foundational text of the Kabbalah; a critical work of Jewish mysticism composed of mystical commentaries on the Torah.

The rue des Aubépines is not a grown-up street, despite her sixty years of urban agitation, for the good reason that she ends in a goat's pecker. She ejaculates, sneezes, sputters and barfs: shacks, jaw harps, and pumice gravel on the empty lot nonchalantly described in *Le monde désert*. A sterile street, but not without interest. It's almost dark. I leaf through my book. "The interlocutor now asks Baladine Nikolaievna, 'But what object were you pursuing?'"[9] One must be weary of the artifices of the interior desert. The brain dries out, the laugh dies while standing, and even genitals lose their colour, their bushes and thorns, if great herds of ideas stop fattening their prairies. Beware Baladine! Then, closing the book and preparing to head toward the lights of the hospital, I read the following lines on the endpaper: The slave, the bald man crouching on his heels like a hen, the tree upturned in an empty sky, the church without a bell tower. All stand for the same thing, the same point of synthesis: the location of the missing phallus.

9 Jouve, *The Desert World,* 51.

The bald man is lying between the undulations of an idiotically green landscape. From the depths of his palace, he observes the high towers with his own wisdom teeth. He thinks of his father. He thinks very often of his father. He dreams of him. Mute, bathing in his own saliva, watchful from his hiding place, kneeling on the mattress of his tongue, the bald man *knows* that he will swallow everything: sperm, bile, and self-esteem as soon as the old serpent visits. His father's penis. But you say a church without a steeple is castrated? In the Col-Vert islands, I remember, churches lack belfries, and these, one foot in the tomb and the other in the soup, await the salt wind under the volcano's smoking eye. Stumps. Calves peeled like onions. Dismembered churches. Deserted women. Sand and ash from five sleepless nights. That's why the bald man is permanently erect: at dawn as at dusk, only candour prevails.

A dead leaf falls on my mouth. Fierce humidity of an awakening mouth. For an entire minute I try to find myself among the rubber rings that surround a fleeting memory. I rise quickly. A book falls. *Le monde désert.* I leave rue des Aubépines in a rush to find "...the necklace that binds us / But who holds the chain?" (Vigny).[10]

I continue on. I follow the palisade, noting the granular neon blue on the naked back of the hospital, a black dog at my side who answers to the almost forgotten name of "Utique," and a new kind of jealousy at my navel.

I let myself fall from the top of the palisade. I have heard that if, when you're sleeping, a snake deep-cleans your ears, once awake, even the language of birds becomes clear. If falling asleep is to fall, what is it to awaken?

---

10 Vigny, Alfred de. *Œuvres complètes: Poésies complètes.* (Paris: Calmann-Lévy, 1893).

The hospital. The heavy nonsense of a pyjama pulled taut over two hips by the high walls of anonymous pain dragging its oily slippers to the shithouse. The patient progresses down the hallway like his illness: without restraint and mostly in reverse. His gown, regulatory as everything else, is gaping. The pyjama also gapes wide over the mossy belly, and so it goes from pocket to pocket, all the way to those dying in the ward, although they are impeccably dressed: asses pursed tightly as old money bags, their clothing, nostrils, eyelids, finally, everything is put to dry and to rest.

"When it's time, they will sneeze in the mirrored wash basin, and then, still tied to life by their mucus and tears, they will dance out their dreams, their woes and their lies... Forty days and forty nights they will clap their lives like castanets in the Grand Hiccup Orchestra: forty days and forty nights to find the shadows, the rose gardens, the bloody and furry roses of paradise lost: the miserly orifice of the maternal belly. And if they don't find it, you say? There are so many false doors in nature... the navel, for example, the viper's nest, certain seas... This is the science of Reversals." Thus speaks the water snake that sleeps between my knees.

It's been ten days since they stopped bringing the newspapers to my room. Breakfast is increasingly rudimentary: a stringy brew with a flotilla of croutons to break the monotony. I reach the final steps leading to the slaughterhouse; they twitch under my footsteps, sleeping as they do, minds elsewhere.

How will I find my father today? Smaller and more birdlike… still recognizable? The night ward seems to say he slept alright. I measure my own relief by the way my heels hammer the indoor sidewalk, the long hallway lined with silent beds. The concrete idea of cold trembles in muddied sheets. Muzzles, buttocks, processions of old men holding their jars of urine connected to their prostates by a thin pink plastic tube, old men, as I was saying, rearing like bridges over their putrid rubble; their waste, corroded, digested, defecated by the anvil, senile, wise, and mad together—all are lining up.

I move forward. The hallways are the hospital's veins, and each patient must dive in, swim against the current, dive into the breaking waves. For every cleared clot, a thousand clots curdle, coagulate, and burst like bubbles. Which one will I be?

On a bench, you listen to a conversation between doctors. A surgeon in a monk's robe speaks with a clear conscience of his latest excavations. For two hours, on another bench located near the neurology lounge, you review the numbers and images of your past and present life. One must pass this boiling time between a commode chair and an electric one, fill the cracks of continuous time with a few pointed taunts, reflections on *bad* weather, memories in a tin: any nonsense, as long as it helps to cross the bridge of mental illness.

The hospital elevator is an ominous mode of transportation. The operator—either a religious dignitary or a member of the Academy—loudly names the signs of certain illnesses he thinks he recognizes on our faces, illnesses typically treated by specialists. The operator doesn't listen to the dreamer who tries to attract his attention by raising his voice, believing, I suppose, that the message must be spoken in a certain way to be received. At seven o'clock in the evening, the Micheline train's horn shrieks as it leaves the tracks. I remember the judgement of another week's elevator operator: the best patient is the one who has the gift of being forgotten in the trenches. Better to undergo an amputation in December than an improvisation in June... I scream out my floor number with the rest of the other prisoners. It seems the elevator operator takes a few requests at random then, ceding to violent emotions, bends his knees, pushes the buttons, and the elevator rises or falls in a nimble or provocative way, depending on the dose of albumen in his cell tissues.

The elevator. A small crowd, made up of doctors in tennis attire and nurses, secretly hostile under a sugar-candy exterior, drifts through the hall in a cloud of laundry soap and gathers beside me in the metallic box. I see myself, pressed on all sides, my nose and my breasts growing, excremental, enormous. The faster the rise, the heavier the transported bodies. The ego stroking of the medical corps causes the elevator operator to ejaculate into a kettle pilfered from the common room for this purpose. Upon arrival, a sensation of dilation, ovarian and testicular expansion, glues the passengers to the walls of the elevator. The operator holds his staff in hand, ready to drill holes into the walls like a termite in case the cabin lacks air. Sixth floor. I exit the elevator, happy to no longer be part of this lewd purée.

For the stiffs, the hospital is a dangerous place, dirty, sad, unsettling, but for the doctor, this same place is no more than a field for a professional football player. The visitor knows the weight of the ritual, of the postal and rectal shakedowns, the impetus of the hours spent on rhino legs, mercilessly crushing the eyelids of the children of the vine; no doubt he is familiar with the stress of not finding things the way he thought he left them the night before: the patient, the bed, the room... the patient might be the same, but the bed? The room?

The heat radiating from the wounds haloes the hospital with a strange green glow. During the day, an always-fresh layer of whitewash hides the graffiti from those for whom despair has long become ordinary. At dawn, when everything is silent except for the ringing in their ears, the notion of captivity swaddles the sallow foreheads of the sick.

The mad woman raises her skirts, lets her hair down, exposes herself. It's time for collective masturbation.

I spend my days sitting on a chair, at times in the room, at others in the hallway. In a friendly meeting, they hand out drinks and food. Doctors rarely offer drinks, sometimes cigarettes, never sex. The sick, sprawled on Carrara marble tiles, stew in their fat, dissolving in it, thus imitating, even in their dreams, the technical and theoretical jargon of their practitioners.

The sick prefer to eat sitting down. "It will be cold," says the cancer patient to his wife, who, glued to her perch, can't stop staring at the clock. "Hang in there," she murmurs once she's free. Her husband watches her leave, weaving with ease through the bloody horde of wounded on her path, her hips agile, legs sheathed with silk.

"They'll never get me," says the cancer patient for the thousandth time and grabs his spur as though to defend himself. "I would refrain from such thoughts if I were you," advises the engineer confidentially. "Says you," retorts the cancer patient. "Do you see the blond intern? The cross-eyed one who makes splendid butterflies with his own waste? Well, I confronted him head-on with my problem. I told him I would never go under the knife, never... too old. All of this, I told him, is working just fine, so best not to tinker."

"And what did he say?" The room has an insatiable desire to bring to light the most tedious old stories.

"Back to the wall. He pushed me back against the wall, and he said, 'As a doctor I should try to carve you up; but as a man, or better yet, as a future patient, I understand your position.'"

"That's just advertising for another hospital," says another patient, blowing his nose into the sink. He holds his nose between his thumb and index, and without even meaning to, the eyes of the ward follow the procession of jellyfish going with the flow, soft, green, iridescent, like oysters without shells, opals. "That's how the Russians entered Prague," says my father. I finished *Le monde désert*. On the last page I read, "He rarely writes, even though there is so much paper in front of him; a crossed-out word on a page means he crumples the paper and starts again. He can't read literature, can't stand the sight of books, becomes particularly ignorant. What he sees in front of him: things, houses, the inanimate, the sky. How he lives: sometimes he works. How he gets money: no idea. He has to wait. Is he getting ready to die? Probably."[11]

No rudimentary person feels as much legitimate aversion to a fetish as I do to this book: this paragraph describes exactly how I feel, my inability to concentrate, and my sketchy occupations; but that last line... shit.

Tonight, I summit my mother's amputated breast. It was bound to happen. The dog dreams of fish, the fisherman also dreams of fish, which does not mean that the fish the dog dreams of are really fish; they could symbolize the drowned man's phallus (the one lost by Osiris, dismembered by

11 Jouve, *The Desert World*, 123.

his brother and haunting the fertile Nile to this day), the Christ. I consider the symbolic significance of fish in early Christianity, or the memory of a badly digested bone. If the fish symbolizes man's phallus: the breast symbolizes the penis. But the amputated breast is doubly forbidden—long live the death of cancer!

Tired and demoralized, I struggle to keep my balance. I shuffle in small steps toward the poorly ventilated interns' room. I hear the slow, very slow hiss of my wet plaid slippers becoming threadbare on the hospital tile. A horrible thought: the word "hospitality" must come from "hospital"! The shrill voices of visitors scatter among the beds and punctuate the tide with a clear note quickly tarnished by the groans of the sick. The chocolate-covered ward girls chase the tent pole under the cardiac patients' camphor-infused blankets—yes, they hunt with hounds, these candied chestnut girls from Martinique. Splashed with blood, they trap the caribou in the common rooms. Woe betides he who thinks himself wild and free, they will gorge on his gangrene, there on his hospital bed, without even asking for permission from the doctor. Suicidal madness is written on a few bodies: an anus sighing after the touch of mud, the catarrhal expulsion of sperm by a collapsed phallus, the gaze from a shifty eye running onto the pillow, all patients pay their dues to the night.

"Piss falls from the sky!" screams the old man stuck in the shitter. "It's raining cats and dogs," says the anglophone with tuberculosis, happy to let his riddle slip, even for a moment. "I have a lake in my belly," whispers the North African, closing his eyelids with finality, like an iron curtain.

"In the trough of the wave, who dares speak of a melancholic tide," answers the cancer patient folding his covers down to his heels like a gambler revealing his four aces.

"It's a question of livestock," says Mr. Cooper, tapping the wall with his slipper in the vain hope that it will quiet the old dog in the room next door. I leave. It seems useless to insist. The old man, sick or not, just like the dog "returns to his vomit," always returns to his own genitalia. He exposes himself, and except for a few fleeting regrets, does so with glory and good spirits. Nevertheless, the public hostility is great: even the most hardened stomachs turn when faced with the white worms and crevasses of the sprawling senility. If, by chance, a visitor or a patient from another species forgets themselves amongst the elderly, they can expect neither protection, nor rest, nor justice: they must go through with it and determine, after careful examination, who amongst the venerated must take the lead, and who should bring up the rear. The zeal of the senile is so vivid and their taste for the shameful so sharp, it's almost impossible to escape. Despotism is everywhere. Everywhere crutches stand in the way. The gates of social class and good manners, insurmountable elsewhere, turn to dust when the patriarch brandishes his sword or grandmother applies make-up to her ass. The need to show off is so strong that even the doctor aspires to it, thinking that maybe if he ridicules their pain enough, it can be pushed aside.

At the slightest flower on the slopes of Taormina, at the slightest crotch zipper dilated by the breeze, at the smallest arabesque drawn by the trembling sex of an old dodderer, I run back to bed and sleep.

Yes, I'm leaving. In the hallway, I go against the current. I take the elevator. I go up or down, my heart too heavy to know which.

I find my room, any room, and almost without undressing, I fall asleep.

Yesterday, on my return, S. opened the fridge, which promptly overflowed. The room is as ugly as a bank, stinking of detritus, filled with liquid. The urine evaporates. The urine, yellow frost on the walls of my room, freezes and faints as my dream perspires. I wonder, vaguely concerned, "And the thaw?"

Later in the morning, I am on a beach surrounded by people of both sexes. A turbulent cloud hurtles like a racing elephant. General panic. I find myself sitting on S.'s lap in an old black automobile which is very high and very black. (My grandmother had a similar car, except hers was red.) The cloud advances unceremoniously over the sand, into the dunes. Teenagers run in clusters, laughing before the storm. "The abyss calls the abyss," says a strange voice coiled in my ear. I think I see the spirit of Théophile Gautier jumping on the shore. Someone throws a buoy or a seagull at the old car. The cloud is back on the offensive. I try in vain to close the car's rear window. I crank the old-style handle; my breasts shake and churn the butter of my blouse. S. sings a few verses of his own making. I crank the handle (S.'s sex?), the window closes stiffly. S. sings and the glass flops down (obvious pun, alas) leaving an opening approximately two fingers wide. The ballooning cloud arrives. It invades the whole scene. Its whiteness seems excessive, toxic. I try, with more success, to keep the window really closed. It's at this point I realize in horror that S. is sitting on the roof of the car; only his legs, hanging like hams (hamstrings; phallic reminder) are still inside. The cloud surrounds us. He is inside and outside. The street dissolves under my eyes and the wheels of the car sink into the swamp. Into snot. The legs fall on the front seat like parentheses. (Protheses?) Awakening. We say, "Open the parentheses." Open the parenthetical legs; judge the tree by its fruit, the dawn, rather than the dead of day... "You talk like a prostitute," says my father.

A year after having transcribed this dream, I read the following in *Violoncelle qui résiste*[12] by Pierre Bourgeade: "I'm at the top of a mountain. I watch the clouds below. They rise. When they reach me, I will die. They aren't clouds, but gas. I can't run. They reach me. I awaken." I remember that this fragment is part of an interview I had with Pierre Bourgeade in 1970. It was published in *La Quinzaine littéraire*[13] and has been republished in a book with twelve similar works. I had completely forgotten that interview, and the dream, to the point of repeating it, image by image, without recognizing it belonged to another. Plagiarism or bad joke?

12 Bourgeade, Pierre. *Violoncelle qui résiste.* (Paris: E. Losfeld, 1971).

13 A bimonthly publication founded in 1966 by Maurice Nadeau and François Erval, known since 2013 as *La Nouvelle Quinzaine littéraire*.

In the morning, I exit the elevator like a kite catching the wind off a cliff. I am hit with the depravity of the place: twelve orderlies, as hysterical as flies on feces, sweep pustules, hip-piss-cus, capsules, legendary foreskins with fast flow, prefixes with *ur*. Some turn in one direction, some in another. Fleeting bees, blushing under the regulatory corolla of their white skirts, their bare bums glimpsed or deciphered at each stop make the elevator climb higher than usual. Dreams are often connected to illness. So here, at the hospital, in the very heart of illness, how does one separate the wheat from the chaff? First, one must draw a line between the horse and the rider. (The horse = the scheme = the dream. Who, then, is the rider?)

This morning, around eight o'clock, the head nurse, or the "matron" as the English say, came to check on my health. I was sitting, like in a classroom, on the bench that faces the window in the hallway. On this bench was an old man with a white beard, a houndstooth cap on his head. He was crying, his head resting on the back of his hand, which was pressed on a cane chair. He was crying as he watched without seeing me. "You don't recognize me, but I am your father," he said, swaying his head.

"I have had no father since I've been here. I feel as though I've become a machine," I answered, not giving it much thought because the matron's large, jewelled chest was blocking my view.

The matron is the paragon of nurses: radiating good health, her sex as frank and open as a can of sardines, she seems straight out of a page from the Old Testament. "I want to sit on your lap," she told me.

No use wasting time with awkward flirting. I kicked the old man in the shins to make him leave and swallowed the matron's prattling tongue.

Suddenly, turning regretfully away from the mirror where she could see herself half-naked on my lap, exposed to the amused glances of the sick, she rose and said: "We aren't going to spend the rest of our lives in a hallway. Let's stop educating the masses like this. Look at this place! How could we even have imagined making love on this bench? What are you doing here? You're nuts, but I'm the head nurse—I don't belong in this dump. We need to find the exit." She jumped up, mercilessly snatching my hand from her moist and wiggling sex: the starfish of a slippery rock, covered in seaweed, glorious like a moist twat. I grabbed her by the waist. Mr. Cooper removed the nurse's skirt, her tights, and military underpants. A patient with scaled glasses massaged the plump cheeks while showing them to the room with pride. "Get to work," Mr. Cooper panted, sitting astride the sprawled flesh. "When there's enough for two, there's enough for three," shouted the bearded man joyfully as he liberated the matron's armoured breasts.

Mr. Cooper stroked the clitoris. I stroked the clitoris. But above all, the bearded man stroked the clitoris with his beard. The matron, kneeling on the bench, her skirt solidly moored to the latch on the door, arched her spine to free her breasts and forgot to protect her ass from the onslaught of patients, tousled with joy. I felt constrained to benefit from her generosity for the well-being of my friends. Such reinforcements! The bench groaned beneath the weight of the matron's grazers. A man snuck under her stomach and gripped her sprawling legs valiantly: his arms, like crutches, held the woman's pelvis. A few forearms slid between her thighs, then some eels and a silver tongue. The prone man nibbled the velvety slit above him, while the bearded man, a little overwhelmed by the events, fondled an addict's right breast. A very old Chinese woman sucked the bearded man's dick, her eyes closed as she pictured herself at church. My breasts, overheated by innumerable pant zippers, flashed in the fog. I tried to get the most out of the strange new bonds of friendship tying me to the matron and the other patients.

Around eleven o'clock, a sick man named Anastasia was killed at the barber's while his widow wrote her name, alongside Mr. Cooper's, on her inner thigh.

The bearded man tried again. He wore a rubber finger. "This is all routine," he mumbled, rummaging through visitors' bags, folders, and the nooks and crannies of the matron's vagina. He tried to explore the addict's anus but had to content himself with the throat of one of the Chinese patients.

"Polio?" asked the bearded man, wiping his glasses. Then after a few moments of silence, he opined: "It's an illness like any other!"

"A deaf intern," sneered the matron in a weak and non-labialized voice. She no longer fought for her freedom: lying on her back on the ground, having abandoned the bench to the newcomers, she spread her legs even wider. Thick honey ran through her bushy hairs, spasms like sobs shook the upturned lips, swollen, chomped at by so many hot heads. Straight as a piston, the matron's clitoris begged for liberation, but no tongue, not even a Chinese one, would grant it the favour. An interesting phonetic and orthographic association between European and Asian tongues: licking the coral, the stomach, and the bellybutton, clicking while changing the fricative consonant of V into the explosive and corresponding B, but never sufficiently to the taste of the matron's clitoris.

"That's it," said the bearded man briefly, who, after a bit of pounding, had his turn and took the addict from behind.

"Friend, what are you doing? What do you do for a living?" asked the matron, her mouth full.

"I do nothing but study tongues," said the bearded man.

"Which tongues?" asked an immigrant sodomizing his brother at the other end of the hallway.

"French, German, and Russian."

"It's all Hebrew to me," said the Chinese man, seemingly impressed.

The matron, ever more perplexed, seemed like a wild beast. A thousand cocks, flags at half-staff, charged on command. The bearded man, supercharged by the addict, masturbated with a syringe. Mr. Cooper orchestrated the patients' pleasures while watching the matron from the corner of his eye to prevent her from coming. "It's cruel to thwart her like this," shouted Salonique,[14] passing through the fray, dreamily rubbing her supervisor's pubis with the palm of her hand.

"Not yet, not yet," begged the addict who, straddled by an Englishman, lent her mouth to a mysterious child.

---

14 Salonique, the French name for Thessaloniki, Greece's second largest city, was home to one of Europe's largest Jewish majority populations before WWII, ninety percent of whom were murdered in the Holocaust.

"Rub and rotate with a double standard," shouted Mr. Cooper while sticking his tongue between a new mother's hanging lips.

The matron groaned with pleasure. Her wound flew through the air, acid labia majora hemming without breaking on the shore, naked, delivered to the prickling, the light touches, and explosions of passersby.

We hid the offending bodies as best we could (the matron's defiled body was the most unwieldy: four people, including myself and Mr. Cooper, sat on it). "Finish me off," she told me point-blank once the assistants were gone. But, satiated, the sick began untangling themselves from one another, trying to flee the fleshy woman and her cumbersome orgasm. "Finish me off, you who started it all," said the matron with tears in her eyes. I climbed onto her stomach. Two patients, one Chinese, the other maimed, held her pelvis. Slowly, I cut off all communication.

Two old men jumped on my back, riddling my butt with their crayons; in their impatience, their aim was too high, but what does it matter? A Maltese man dripping with snot sunk his dagger between my thighs, then, sneezing joyfully, ringed his scrotum into the addict's anus.

"Finish me!" screamed the matron, "My nerves are shot."

Mr. Cooper burst into his habitual laughter, and using a razor blade, divided the dissenting clitoris in two. "I'm sorry," he said, "that's Salomon's[15] judgement."

I emerged from my reverie in time to see the exquisite sight of the head nurse in evening dress closing the door of my cell.

Six o'clock in the evening. When I'm depressed, the sun sets in the sewer.

15 French spelling of Solomon.

The first day, seeing that I looked lost, an intern told me, "At the hospital, we can tell the visitors from the sick by the way they cross their legs." Since then, I watch the wind bend clitorises in fields of grey flannel, and I close the doors of my soul to pity. You must be tough as a nurse to return to solid ground. Every night, before going to sleep, I touch the ground twice on each side of the bed. In dreams, I prowl under the arbutus trees accompanied by radiologists, who, with sleeves and eyelids rolled up, swig their soup in tubs meant for washbasins.

There are many German quarters in Geneva and, the hospital being the spitting image of the city, many quarters of German meat in the morgue.

Full of merit, yet poetically
Man dwells on this Earth.
HÖLDERLIN[16]

16 Hölderlin, Friedrich. *Hölderlin: Selected Verse*, trans. Michael Hamburger. (London: Anvil Press Poetry, 1986).

The hospital's productions are not the least of its mysteries. They consist of such a variety of forms and substances that it tortures the minds of naturalists. Is this matter from the kingdom of animals or plants? Is it formed by living creatures? Or is it something in between? In general, mammals have scent glands not just in their genital regions, but also in the hollows of their armpits.

Les Halles.[17] I've always spun on jealousy's roasting spit. A horde of women, laughing their heads off, pack and unpack my suitcase on the tiles. Grasshoppers. They pull the cover toward them, unmasking the naked ground of my secret thoughts. So many unmade beds, so much unpacking in a woman's head. My red suitcase empties as I try to fill it with old newspapers. Women, with golden incandescent eyes, give a slight sway of their rear ends while passing the head doctor. They decorate the big, deserted bed: the belly of Paris. Spreading their glitter, their tears, their rubies, on the sheets and pillow. My pillow. I get close to see better.

17 Les Halles was Paris's former central fresh food market, housed in iron-and-glass pavilions, which inspired Émile Zola's *Le ventre de Paris*. They were demolished in 1971.

The ambassador of Great Britain's socks bask there comfortably. (Might it be a discrete allusion to a sinister memory of capotes anglaises?)[18] A silver serpent lifts its tail in recognition of authority. The sick, after all this hullabaloo, will often start to clean each other. A stiff rope strangles the neck of the penis tightrope walker. Only waking dreamers can operate without a net.

I hook my ear onto the lock of life: a truck passes under my windows. I breathe. Everything has been pre-arranged. I just need to raise my hand, turn on the light, or swear by any stupid thing to be definitively free. I slip the rope around my neck, fall asleep, and the dream continues.

The same grinding mechanisms, the same protagonists, with just a bed. Exposed on the bedsheet, my "family jewels" sparkle like a martyr on his shroud, or a glittering moth pinned at all four corners.

Sea wing. A large shell that finishes with a scream. His byssus, or beard, is as soft as silk. A doe shell. Why a doe? Perhaps due to the watchful presence behind the door? Word plays and meanderings: antlers, passing the buck, cloven hooves, crowbar, porte-cochere, dummy door, kosher cut, side aisles, the burr under the saddle, etc.

The ambassador tries to embrace me. Embarrassment in the ambassador's embrace. I rebuff him despite my budding love. Then, finding that the animal of the diplomatic corps has swollen once and for all, and that my refusal will only fuel his desire, I tell myself: "Ah, if only in life I could deny myself like this..."

Scene change. I'm watching a hunt. I am both the hunter and the hunted. A large stag rears, his antlers blazing in the

18 Capotes anglaises: A French term for condoms from the 1950–60s, meaning "English coats" or "English hoods," comparable to the British term "French letters."

clearing, his stiff legs working the snow. The feast of nausea now begins in me.

The stag charges twice. A voice foretells the third and fatal charge. "Kill him," orders the ambassador. "You, like the rest of your kind, you're a good shot. Kill this stag." It seems to be the gun chosen by the British man. I am the stag on my knees. I am the hunter standing. I am the spilled blood. I am the penis and the earth. (Sharp shooters shoot swiftly... shoes? ...André?) Here I leave the realm of desire, seen through the body of another, through the double reversal of roles: the stag becomes a camel.

Those familiar with the camel's habits avoid its bite. The tops of its teeth are a dirty olive colour, and the undersides are silvery. It's clear just from hearing it, that the animal is drowning in its own saliva. I stand dreamily in front of the crouching animal, having removed my cap out of respect. I hear someone say: "Cut its throat. It's customary," and despite the clamours, the camel is slaughtered.

A castrating dream? A stag is a bachelor in English. It's common knowledge that the camel, with its penis facing inward, can only make love back-to-back. Regardless of the partner?

A moment later I am again locked in the mouth of my entrails: a conger eel who swallows another eel… to an old dance tune. At the foot of my bed, an old woman tied to her chair by luggage straps cries and laments like a professional mourner. Not far from there, pretty nurses from Martinique and Salonique (a ward assistant who prefers to wash the dishes rather than care for the sick) play at extracting money from a badly hidden purse under a mattress. Grey tears fall from the eyes of the sedentary antiquity: "I want to leave. I beg you, call my husband, tell him I'm ready, tell him I want to leave, that he should come get me. Everyone is waiting for me at home." It's a new tone, as surprising in its novelty as Mr. Cooper's new hat. "Sure, sure," laugh the idiots, "Tickle, tickle. To the circus, old bat!" Stunned by their cruelty, I lean toward the wrinkled face: "I'll call him. I promise. How can I find your husband?"

The old woman looks at me as though I've just been shot by William Tell. She says nothing. She cries. Little furrows chap her skin like acid indentations. I stand back up, uneasy, unable to bear the smell of seated senility any longer.

The Martinican puts me back to bed. I notice she's reading *Le démon de la solitude.*[19]

"No one can help her," hiccups the nurse.

"Yes, please, I'm ready, I want to leave. Help me. Tell my husband to come get me," cries the old woman.

"The phone number... I have a pen and paper... I'll get it... tell me the number?"

"Her husband's been dead for over forty years," says Salonique, preventing me from leaving my bed. The old woman's eyes flood the whole hallway with thick, yellow dust. The wet felt of a minute of silence weighs on my tongue.

"Call him. You promised me," the old woman whimpers into her handkerchief. My brain insinuates all kinds of dirt. I don't know what holds me back from throwing her out the window, that vermin and her chamber pot. Tomorrow I will lower my gaze. I will go on my way. Better to laugh about it, when the neighbour dies. To laugh so as not to die. Laugh or die? A simple shift in mood. Come to think of it, "Oum" is the divine breath of Genesis, the Word in a way. "Oum" sounds like "doom."

But I digress. The eroticism of the elders is not the goal in question.

---

19 Galzy, Jeanne. *Les démons de la solitude*. (Paris: Ferenczi, 1937). In the original French of "Floating Islands," Mansour misspells the title as singular.

Motionless near the rudder that is my father's member, I watch through dream the slumber of a very young man. He looks like me. Mr. Cooper endlessly drags himself like a corpse on the upper deck. "He *thinks* he's sleeping," he tells me half scientifically, half amused. The cancer patient runs counterclockwise: "Doctor, doctor, come quickly, the simulator is dead." I let go of the rudder that is my father's penis, it's become exasperating, especially as my father is getting the hang of it. He plays the same endless game. First the right hand: forte fortissimo. Then the left: forte allegro. Then both: fortissimo, suavissimo, electrissimo. Faster and faster. He doesn't need me to lend him a hand. He takes the rhythm down a notch, then rebuilds, piece by piece, lento, forte, left, right. While the exact purpose of an orgasm is still debated, there is a large consensus in Swiss hospitals on the nutritive function of some forms of masturbation.

Everything stops. Mr. Cooper, his plaid bathrobe open as a parenthesis, drops a brief and dirty laugh like a woodcock stew. My father hangs his member on a nail. "The simulator is dead, you say?" No one dares believe him. Who is sleeping now?

This is how secret laws of nesting periods for ideas are born. The whirlwind survives the passage of the stone, like a notion, a pendulum that has stopped swinging.

The Lobby. It's four o'clock in the afternoon and I stole a chair, an aspirated *h* like that of Van Gogh. Salonique, a wooden bar placed across her chest, snaps her fingers, clicks castanets, punctuating the silence with her sneezes and small whimpers: she knows it's time for English tea, time for a languid nap in the shade of the bamboos and mangroves, but also time where death rages amongst the kneeling sick and the wild beasts. I move my chair, my aspirated *h*, unaccustomed to phonetic changes. A door opens. The hallway, like a rolling sidewalk of triumphant illness, carries the bearers of sullied dreams up to their knees, the inveterate smokers on their cigar-shaped crutches, the scum of fate. Here, everyone smokes, even the most out of breath. Salonique is quiet now. The doctor receives the sick on his couch. We can moan, smoke, howl, smoke, curse, cajole, do whatever we want... he listens. We pour our melancholy into his immense ear and the smoke, our thoughts in uniform, carries away what's left.

I am nervous. I scratch myself. My nails are immediately covered in ground meat. Ten minutes of silence. A door opens swiftly. It's my turn.

"The navel is a false door. A closed door, like a fortified city," whispers the nurse to reassure me.

"Lie down on the table," says the gloved doctor stuffing a few thousand bills into his pocket.

"He's going to examine me without even washing his gloves!" I think, terrified.

"These gloves are procedural," he says nonchalantly in response to my unarticulated question. "Custom officials wear them to conduct searches." This could be an explanation of my dreams about my badly belted, or bloodied, suitcases. What about the camel?

There is noise coming from the corridor. I regularly stick my head out of my lair three times a day, and seven times on days of medical visits, just to air out the room. For now, the corridor is a great, dried-up river bed. I sink my head into my shoulders and the infernal round between the bed and the washbasin begins again. The chamber pots perform the saraband with the drip bulb. The cancer patient's pyjamas kneel in each puddle of blood; the wet flaps of the vest unveil a rich spaniel mane. The stripes, embedded in the cleft that separates the buttocks, seem to vibrate like those of a zebra. Two reservoirs of rosé saliva overflow. Two spittoons per cancer patient. Two chamber pots under each livid window. How can I burst the abscess of resentment that swells in my chest? What forceps will pull disgust from my mouth? Outside, the weather is beautiful, birds sing, the granite air washes its feet in the lake. But here, in the room, no one dares put down the poisonous shrub other than beneath the bed sheets. "No one knows if the fruits are edible," whispers Mr. Cooper, leaning his cheek on my shoulder. A giant wave of nausea swallows us both, a tidal wave of rage, shit, and vomit. I sniff the undergrowth, half-way between the erection of these mysterious monoliths labelled “women’s desires” and a total blackout. Luckily for me, my assailant lets go, putting down the porcelain receptacle that he was holding behind his back, and saying with a dignified look: “I don’t feel well.” “Me neither,” I say, realizing how he plans to use his chameleon tongue: a meat fly assails the Martinican’s cheeks crowned with soot as she leans over a bed. My fingers strike Mr. Cooper’s ribs like a pianist touching a piano. A Hebrew expression flows without rolling or vulgarity between his used lips. What if his thorax caved under the pressure of my thumbs? “Ships that pass in the night,” the moribund whispers in English in my ear. I finally know the identity of the person with the largest sounding probe.

Read before falling asleep: an essay by Dominique Fernandez in *Incidences de la psychanalyse*,[20] where Van Gogh's chair is the topic of discussion. It is written: "The two chairs are empty; the emptiness symbolizes the longing for death. The other chair belongs to Gauguin and represents Van Gogh's dead father." I dreamed I sat in one of those chairs.

The burning sensation isn't a snare, but the pain between my thighs caused by the lost ear certainly is.

20 Pontalis, Jean-Bertrand, ed. "Introduction a la psychobiographie" in *Incidences de la psychanalyse: Nouvelle Revue de la psychanalyse*. (Paris: Gallimard, 1970).

I get a letter:

Dear Friend,

According to Nietzsche, the friend is always the third wheel to the anchorite.[21] *It is because I don't consider you to be just anyone that I allow myself to address you as such. I have been asked, even ordered, to write a few words about myself. This is a bit awkward. It is indeed delicate and indelicate to speak of oneself. I've heard friends in the regiment say too many times, "Spare me your life story," to feel the desire to write it all down. In order to be worthy of a biography, one must have lived like Saint Teresa of Ávila. First, let me inform you that I am* not *Mr. Cooper...*

Now, my life is the sea. An internal storm tossed me out, and while wandering along the shore, I saw an oyster yawning out her life. I took her, and she became my wife. Inside, lacquered, moist, was a pearl. It was at Cancale that we met. We named

21 Nietzsche, Friedrich. *Thus Spake Zarathustra: A Book for All and None*, trans. Thomas Common, Project Gutenberg, 10 Apr. 2023.

our daughter Pascale, so that she could be as soft as the lambs who graze peacefully at the foot of the Mont Saint-Michel. When I was her age, ten years old, or so I'm told, because a child could never pretend to be any other but the golden age, I wanted to be a sailor. My uncle Thaddée would have been a grade above admiral if he hadn't left the navy for business. He always knew how to steer his ship, and with good reason—his mother was English. Her maiden name, which I know by heart, was Iris Parker. She loved all things beautiful. She loved me so much; I never understood why.

I called her Mémé. We took tea together. Then I steered off course. I loved the sea mother, and grandmother, who returned my love. But me, I gave it all back to the sea. The sea, so alive: she comes and goes like that movie from yesterday (which they show today at the hospital). I can sing "in the distance, the sea has retreated"[22] *and add that from the bottom of my heart, grandmother has retreated. In short, my dream of becoming a sailor went down the drain. The sea was solitude; since I'm not at sea, my thoughts are flighty. Only death kills.*

Signed: COOPER

The author of this letter withers on the vine a couple beds over from mine. He is clearly pained and disappointed to see me holed up in my illness and sends me back to other days. I seek Austin Cooper's gaze. Still under the spell of that sublime puppet show put on by the bearded man and the matron, I don't dare ask any questions. I think I understand: I am accepted; I can stay. In short, healing through our own kind.

22 Prévert, Jacques. "Sables mouvants" in *Paroles* (Paris: Gallimard, 1946).

Full of envy, I ask the guard standing in front of me, pale and flat in his nurse's gown, as useless as a politician in a perfume shop: "I wish to see a manager."

"Come back later!" he says with the greatest distress. "Come back when I will have gotten my orders."

I comply, swimming against the current: "But... How will I know...?"

The guard says, urgently, "Don't tell anyone I told you to come back. Just pretend you've come by chance!"

No one dares interrupt the young interns' painful games. In the venomous ward, I remember begging for advice from a blond intern: "What must one do to be seen by Professor Muller? I read his name downstairs, by the staircase, on some kind of honour roll."

The young man raised his heavy eyelids, and pulling away with disgust, answered: "You can't ask such a thing." He was moulting! The harrowing flight of the nurses, the yellow spots on his crocodile shoes: everything confirmed my diagnosis, he was moulting!

I felt brave, the focal point of so many hopes: "And why not?"

"Because Professor Muller never steps foot in the hospital."

"You mean to tell me that the venerable head with long grey hair only exists in my mind?" I didn't want to lose my hope in the senile. I needed to believe in this Professor Muller: "Isn't he in charge of the sixth floor?"

"Yes, of course. All the old, whether sick or not, are his children."

"And despite this he never comes to visit us?" My voice was shaking like the postman after the ball.

"He reads your files." Long live the barbers of yesteryear!

A horde of feelings rises in me. I remember the old Dr. Rosenberg, his nasal voice, his tuberous hands, kneaders of prepubescent stomachs... the way he had of forcing you to tell him your heartbreaking certainties while tickling your butt with his salt and pepper beard. It's always on prison walls that one scribbles words of hope. It's been a long time since old Dr. Rosenberg straightened his knees between his patients' thighs; he floats eternally between two stools facing the unmade bed of the sandy Mediterranean. One blue and gold afternoon at Sidi Bishr No. 2 (a trendy beach near Alexandria), with enough wind to make the dust boil, I found the body of the old doctor while I was out for a swim. I turned over his heavy, listless body. I brought it back to the surface thinking it was a buoy or an old rubber boat. He seemed overcome by a magic slumber. I called frantically for help without letting go of my attending physician's flaccid stomach, leaning on him as if he were a raft. No one heard me. A surge of children's voices gave me the strength and the courage to cast off the corpse... I even resumed my clumsy breaststroke. The old Dr. Rosenberg seemed to glide; he trailed me effortlessly, as if passionately drawn to me. He placed his gelatinous hand on my shoulder like a crêpe; his legs prevented me from advancing, his head rose to the surface. I pushed him away with terror and disgust. His complacent, fawning attitude; his leech-like ways; his weight, like a camel filled to the brim... he horrified me. I was about to sink. To swallow. I gave a final kick in the direction of the drowned man's balls, who, faithful as a poodle, had his arms around my neck. Miracle or indigestion? The drowned man spat up a piece of melon and released me. I swam backward as if in a dream, and the old Dr. Rosenberg, crying like a drunk cow, sank furiously into the abyss.

Dr. Bayer is also dead. Eager for new discoveries, he wiped the slate clean on our girlish escapades without having to be begged. "Get undressed," he would yell at pig-snouted spectators haunting his vestibule. He rummaged our sensitive areas from cellar to gables, sculpted in our frieze. The doctor's pink tongue completed his investigation when the scalpel of the man in white forced you to arch your spine. "You see, the ones with the red pompoms? They were gifts from the navy," he would shout triumphantly, one finger on the brink of the anal orifice, the other stretched tight toward the fired-up crowd. Everything was false and deep and true at once. We let ourselves be devoured by Dr. Bayer without considering we were playing a part: we would spread our legs with volcanic furor before the old fool. "The latest nonsense," simpered the young lady from the post office, who was fond of the show and often just "passing by."

They're all dead, these old doctors, and those who have taken their place, so alike in their youth, are nothing more than a pile of trash.

I am starting to understand the renunciation of the self, prescribed with varying degrees of clarity by all religions.

The suppression of penchants, starting with the basest ones. Detachment. To abstain (ab-stain?) from love. Erase hatred, even forget friendship. The world is not the same for different people; it is the same only when it is deprived of life or when our relationship to it is deprived of life. Like the scream unleashed in the illogical forest of the hospital, like its echo outside. Listening to the answers, the screamer can discern if his scream is right or wrong. I ab-stain from my courage. I am no longer coquettish, nor done up, nor washed on certain days. I ab-stain from my past. I no longer try to run. Chance no longer even has any importance; it falls into banality as soon as it appears. First, are we not here to display our vices and flaws, our extraordinary uniqueness? No one has time to listen to the neighbour; no one even wants to look at him. Without awareness, without tension or confusion; without a phone call to friends, chance loses its charm. It no longer moves us. We forget it.

I give up trying to understand why I'm here. I leave the question open. I've liberated my entourage from my ghost: I know that "outside" visits are considered tedious. I no longer receive any. I no longer read. I no longer write. I wait.

Christ crucified between two thieves: one negative, one positive, one negative. I often think about the invisible border between (so-called) Good and Evil. Extremes touch each other, apparently. Mr. Cooper does too.

Naïve in their freshness, beyond Voltaire's grasp, the *yes* and the *no* continue between the lines of my thoughts. My head is their temple. (In English, "temple" means "place of worship" or "side of the forehead.") The *yes* first: positive, joy, continuity; then, without warning, the *no*: negative, disjointed, death. (A very distinct feeling of suffocation.)

The hallway sucks up my days like an intestine does wool. The elevator vomits clots of eight or ten people on the green carpet of the lobby. Large waves of sleep swell and sway between the stairwell and the common rooms. The *yes* and the *no* swarm my brain, follow each other, and multiply, separated by a thin membrane: the skin of my face. (This is why I no longer wear makeup.) They're trying to unite. I'm afraid of waking to a resounding *no*. The absence of love. Decompression. The trough of the wave. Then the climb back up, the corpse abandoned on the embankment, certainty. I awaken. It's yes-no. Neither *yes* nor *no*. Naturally.

Insomniacs, bowed like dolphins, visit us in our cell-like compartments: "Does anyone know the convoy leader?"

And since no one answers, they continue: "We think he's crazy." The world of the mad is often much more beautiful than that of the living. The fruit of New Caledonian ghost-trees are much more succulent than the real fruit. My mouth is shaped like a gladiolus and probably tastes like one, too: a result of repressing disgust and fear too much, it's lost its nocturnal air.

The common room occupants must cross the hallway on their knees. The double rooms for the most talkative of the bedridden rarely unveil their secrets, but, around four o'clock in the morning, just like the long-haul drivers on the black cobblestones of the North, the Seriously Sick, pale on their stretchers, glide toward the morgue. All those bogged down in the hallway smoke standing up; all those in the way at this hour, each one covers their ears so as not to hear the unctuous wind that flutters the white muslin drapes—death. They belch obscenities. They suck on their cigarette butts, their stumps, or their just deserts. Derisive victory. As Jung says, "Fanaticism is always a sign of repressed doubt."[23]

Shift change. I say with regret: the myth of Swiss cleanliness has a tough skin, but thanks to a pathetic and small caste of ultra-chauvinistic patients whose talk is peppered with racist scraps, the filth, hidden beneath ample Protestant skirts, lifts its head and sees the light of day. Great news: the good old filth from "undeveloped countries" clutters

23 Jung, C. G., *The Symbolic Life: Miscellaneous Writings*, trans. R. F. C. Hull, ed. Herbert Read et al., vol. 18 of The Collected Works of C. G. Jung. (Princeton: Princeton University Press, 1976).

homes, hospitals, and the bland minds of the Helvetii. Just like everywhere else, on Sundays, pastors count the broken eggs, teachers shell the testicles of foreign workers, and someone, somewhere draws hasty conclusions. The filth of ashtrays or chamber pots that are never fully emptied has no equal in my view than that of the grime of a badly stuffed mind. The distressing monotony of the bedsheet pulled up high to hide the sick body, the snore of the milling machine in the neighbour's throat, the unsalted food served in the same basin used for cleaning oneself or for amusement—ennui, mostly ennui, slimy and pernicious—"calm as madmen," says Artaud. I hate lac Léman.

TYPES OF PYJAMAS ENCOUNTERED IN THE LOBBY

The Tidier: Male or undefined. He moves in leaps. His powerful, unretractable claws allow him to tidy furniture or objects, empty ashtrays, etc. Mobile and generating smoke, The Tidier is dangerous because his habit is contagious. His call is very recognizable: "Close the door, please." Suffering from colitis or acute constipation, The Tidier usually engages in protection-type jobs (museums, libraries, banks, parking lots, daycares, etc.).

The Corpulent is an omnivorous, plantigrade mammal. This pyjama, whose junk is indifferent, is a hedonist, a wet blanket, an everyman-for-himself: he could dig his own grave. The Corpulent spends long hours hanging from a telephone wire. Easily domesticated, despite badly concealed predatory tendencies, he devastates attics, soiling the food stores and the literary admirations of his hepatic spit ups; The Corpulent is always in a good mood. He doesn't feel guilt over his desire to empty his mother. He says:

My head is empty
My belly is full

No border guards
Just my throat

Unwanted, he must *take*.

Then there is Mr. Cooper. Grand irrigator of air chambers. "Write: *Mr. and Mrs.*," he screams in English for the benefit of the visiting women who wear wool coats and wide-brimmed hats, "there is no rule preventing dying, unmarried, and legal adults from fornicating." Lying in the west wing of hallway forty-eight, in a windy spot between two Oldsmobiles and a puddle of horse excrement (left no doubt by the mounted police), Mr. Cooper complains to no end. He exposes himself, too. No psychological explanation is necessary or valid: everyone is an exhibitionist after a few days at the hospital, some from bravado, others from couldn't-care-less-ness. The myth follows the established model. Blessed are the nearsighted in these conditions. "Mr. Cooper, your initials." The wretched young nun is farsighted.

Misunderstood until my arrival because he's English, Mr. Cooper has developed a sign language based on his body odours, the colour of his tongue, and the ever-changing length of a horrible Velpeau bandage he's wrapped around his cock. For example, to understand his disdain for The Tidier, Mr. Cooper can either exhibit genital urticaria, a bandaged thigh placed carelessly on a chair, or both. My arrival has caused Mr. Cooper to grow more sombre by the day: I translate his thoughts even before they leave his lips, and nothing soothes his itching limestone rocks anymore.

"Why the devil am I hairy?" I ask myself again today. I was sweeping under the silent bed of the little addict. The clunky wing of the Englishman's blanket was falling from my shoulders without, however, touching the ground. No one entered or exited the elevator. A buck was tirelessly jumping over the fence between the kitchen and the shitter. This is Geneva.

Seeing me pensive, the corpulent man and the Tidier begin to sing:

> The Cadaver must be put away
> Move him so that the others
> Can't eat him
> Eat and tidy
> Chair shards and table runners
> Serpent hills and thunderbirds
> Tidy and eat
> Lickers
> Dryers
> Men with tongues hanging
> Men of the party, hung
> God will handle the remains

"Fuck Margaret Mead," Mr. Cooper says in English.

Every other night, the patient wearing my nightgown announces that she's waiting for Maréchal Juin.[24] Like me, she remembers her name, her address, her age, but her memory stops at the precise moment she arrived at the hospital. I asked her: "Why Maréchal Juin? What do you have against Foch[25] or Pétain?"[26] I had the distinct impression she was suffering from physical pain. I asked if she had slept well: "No, I'm just tired." I had to retreat; the country's most skilled hunters came for her with their large-calibre ammo meant for reluctant game, and their dogs meant for hunting bears or bucks. A grey bus was parked in front of the grand entry to the Morgue: another, filled with masked

24 Alphonse Pierre Juin (1888–1967): Algerian-born senior French army general known for fighting decolonization. He served as the Marshal of France from 1952 until 1962.

25 Ferdinand Foch (1851–1929): French general, Marshal of France, and member of the Académie Française and the Académie des Sciences. He was the Supreme Allied Commander on the Western Front during WWI.

26 Philippe Pétain (1856–1951): French military officer. He commanded the French Army in WWI and became the head of the collaborationist regime of Vichy France during WWII.

men, was making the rounds while shouting down the adjacent streets. “Hitting won't do any good,” whispered my father, who can't stand the sight of someone else's blood. “What if I asked for justice from the great Head Physician?” says Mr. Cooper, elbows on his pillow like Saint Paul reclining on the Apostles ossuary. “What do you want to do with two packs of blond cigarettes?” asked my father. “The Swiss can't be bought so cheaply.” “I can try to lie to him,” says Mr. Cooper without much hope. “He won't believe me, the great Head Physician, but I can always try.” He just had to try.

For one reason or another, a special guard in a pale blue uniform is now stationed at the entrance to the bathroom. Another sentinel checks bags, suitcases, and satchels for all those wishing to assist the embalming workshop at the bottom of the stairs. Yesterday, thinking he was alone, the latter split the angles of the Martinican woman with a saw. He stuck his tongue in her enlarged crack and swallowed the unrepentant clitoris. Suction sounds accompanied the mechanical ascent. “No one avoids getting frisked when I'm on duty,” he said, as if to apologize. It's difficult to recognize the role vertigo plays in his case: from which misalignment does he build his delirium? Besides, even hens mutually help one another in cases of specific danger: one of them swallows half a blade of grass that she can neither swallow nor spit out; she signals her discomfort, and her colleague immediately runs to her aide, plucking the troublesome blade of grass from her beak while managing not to swallow it herself. Apples and oranges, you say? I don't think sentinels are hens: I'm just saying they behave the same way.

We were overpowered by the blue guards. Mr. C. and I were transferred to the bathroom for the entire weekend, and my father played dead so convincingly that he was left unattended without food or water for the same duration. Behind the padded doors, we counted slaps, kicks in the stomach, and teeth ripped out. We learned to eat cheese on slices of soapy bread. Naked, under the eyes of visitors who dismantle you like an object, we evoked a classless society. We were vacationing in the kingdom of anger. No one is more stubborn than the English.

The fourth day, we were released. Then, through the paternal penis, we again penetrated the motherhouse.

Preliminary Work

Countless corpses clutter the embalming workshop, flooding the marble slabs with their thin, clear urine because they've been unhexed, freed, ousted. "We were lovebirds for fourteen years," mumbles Mr. C. passing a corpse. "Rest, rest for eternity, dear old bag." "Pâté for breakfast," says my father.

Something that resembles stained glass from a church appears on the nurses' white aprons, and their red hands, making the sign of the cross on the prone patients' flesh, recall the hosannas of a very young sun. A wingless bird, more crayfish than cassowary, sings the mass. Plainchant: with the unbearable burn of magnesium meant to freshen one's face and the old, flexible rod of the Head Physician to recognize the chosen ones.

Unlike consumptives, spiritists fight death. Western medicine has two ways to treat these rebels, these revenants. The mad ones. We can either bury or mutilate them. There is in fact a procedure for ridding oneself of all types of intruders: exorcism or conjuration. Originally practised by ecclesiastics against demons, exorcism today falls under the regular duties of nurses. The spectre of Athénodore (see Pliny)[27] is delivered after his burial, just like the spirit mentioned in "the friend of lies." (Lucian. II.)[28]

My leg is propped on the windowsill as though it no longer belongs to me. I am probably drugged, and the secret geometry of fear has lost its charm. "Mass is restful," says the cancer patient boldly.

"Shush," says my father. "A male nurse has left a piece of his tongue between my teeth and I'm afraid we might be heard."

"Is it possible to lose a piece of tongue and retain the ability to speak?" asks the surgeon who tries to stick his bits into every conversation without exception.

Upon hearing these words, Hubert, Mr. Cooper's brother who works in administration, climbs on the table and gives a brilliant speech on the authoritative techniques of dental surgery of his youth. Elsewhere, in the South of France, for example, the Mal-Placé dam bursts, causing thousands of deaths in its wake and mass-producing refugees in the region. "Long live the death of General Franco!" yells the cancer patient, a recalcitrant smoker of small, crutch-shaped cigars. He thinks Salonique is Spanish. "He's lost his head," says Mr. Cooper's brother, who hides all the signs of vegetative spasmodic neurosis in the folds of a large bathrobe. "He's lost his legs," laughs the surgeon, brandishing his organ.

Lying in the "visitor's" armchair, hands tucked backward in her belt, Salonique, motionless, watches twilight approach. Her head slides and looks toward the darkness

27 "Athenodorus and the Haunted House," a tale recounted by Pliny the Younger (c. 61–113 CE).

28 Lucian of Samosata (c. 125–after 180 CE): Hellenized Syrian satirist who parodied religion, superstition, and philosophy.

while involuntary movements shake her pelvis. She slowly lifts her skirts, spreading her chatterboxes, unsheathing her suction cups; she shamelessly exposes her wooden barrels, her pickled cucumbers, her lived experience. My father often says that without the pickle, smoked salmon, and saffron rice, the ghetto would be flavourless.

I've managed to establish particularly close contact with a tooth extractor. Yesterday, the cancer patient, Mr. C., and I went to bed without taking a sedative. During the night, a beautiful bass voice thundered in the hallway: "We forced her to bend the knee, it's something." I became rigid and could no longer move, despite my ardent efforts and the unpleasant impression that my legs had been emptied of blood. A room can become a trap for those who defend it, but once on the outside, how naked is the traveller! Mr. C. and the cancer patient seemed plunged in an endless sleep. Knowing them, I wondered if they were only pretending. Better a cage-bed than a grave. The owner of the deep bass came up the central aisle between our beds, which was humid as a ditch in the fall. "I'm eating too much," I thought with repulsion, petrified with disgust. A strange feeling of déjà vu crept over me: kneeling on my chest, a tooth extractor, red but not from anger, was fighting for his life. Fortunately, he was able to insert a toothpick into the massive vagina that faced him without spilling a single drop of seminal liquid. Peace returned to the room.

"I think it's a boy," said the extractor. "Come see for yourself." And he showed me my hidden face in the mirror.

I saw a woman in labour. She opened her mouth, exposing the child nestled in a nook like an egg in its nest... "Breathe," said the extractor (extract her?) studying his future catch. Then, after two minutes of hesitation (did he really have time?), he ditched his trousers and buried his cock in the mouth of the woman who had given birth.

"Here we go! He's sticking his crank back into lust," sneered the cancer patient, turning back to the wall. "Eau de vie," mumbled the extractor next to my ear.

"Fountain of youth, living water," said Mr. C., rushing toward the source.

"Leave me some!" blubbers the new mother with my mouth, squeezing her knees together.

"Run for your life!" howls the extractor, as he heads for the elevator. "The child is safe; may God protect the mother." Leaving the hospital, I am determined to order dentures.

THE NAP

From my bed, I watch Austin Cooper: originally from Birmingham, a freed slave or a spy on the Head Physican's payroll. Outside, the beechwoods and wild palm trees become tinged with russet. In the armchair, Mr. C., bloated, bulging, swollen with fat, silently exposes his penis. It appears that Hippocrates, after Hesiod and Empedocles, understood the impact of a pregnant woman's imagination on the fetus.[29] Mr. Cooper's mother, a strange creature with lidless eyes, frequented a certain Joe—an elephant tamer by trade. What is the relationship between the symmetry of Mr. Cooper's genitals and the wild palm trees? And why do the sexual organs of plants possess symmetrical structures? The ancient Egyptians, exclusively depicted in profile, enemies of chaos and of asymmetry, slip into the chocolate night of great magic: they know that symmetry attracts demons, and they turn the other cheek. Tibetans, however, avoid it.

29 Ancient Greeks theorized the maternal imagination could physically impact the developing fetus.

Let's return to Austin C. I know that his leg is healthy despite the horrible description of its putrefaction posted on the wall above the sink. A nun shares my vigil; together we overlook the patient like marble cliffs;[30] it's not really my fault if the white woollen blanket is stained with blood; the nun has not yet decided to control her auricular period. The reason for the ear hemorrhage zis clear: the famous "blood rushing to the head" from unfortunate memory.

"My hair hurts," she says in a plaintive voice.

"Plug your ears," I say, barely moving my lips. In my eyes, an ear, with or without a pinna, is no more interesting than a vagina.

"It has to bleed," says the nun.

I have the very clear impression that I've moved up a level on the path to awakening: the level of repulsion.

Radin[31] writes (page 138) how a man dreamt about the

---

30 A reference to the short novel *Sur les falaises de marbre (Auf den Marmorklippen)* by German author Ernst Jünger published in 1939, translated into French by Henri Thomas in 1942.

31 Paul Radin (1883–1959): American anthropologist and folklorist specializing in Indigenous cultures and languages, he most notably studied the Trickster figure in Winnebago/Ho-Chunk mythology.

"spirit of thunder": "When he wanted to create lightning, he sang a song praising the spirit of thunder. Then, when he was done, he cut some tobacco and put some in the fire and the rest in his pipe. He then shouted toward the south: 'May there be thunder.' The next day, there would be a terrible thunderstorm." Is this why my father smokes?

We make music with our hands, with our mouths, with our asses, with our lungs, and our brains; but for our genitals, we have no say in the matter. Moreover, what patient over the age of ninety can still brag about being in possession of spermatozoa that live up to their name? As recently as this morning, the stage manager pronounced a brief and mysterious word through the cancer patient's mouth. In his mouth, in his bellybutton, in his anus, and also, with difficulty, because he had very little breath left, in his urethra. We placed a floral partition around the anonymous dying man. It's been almost eight days, and his body boils and smokes without pause; his rattle evokes a yellowish image of religion... He bothers us.

The stage manager turned over the anonymous man's decaying body with the small strokes of a butter churn. He perked up the old concave buttocks with a few strokes of his tongue. From now on, I know, the air of the great night will flow through the window left ajar: the anal path to the moon.

I'm looking for a forgotten name. The standing water of moral decline stagnates under the beds; the memory is hidden in the broom closet or the one with the scalpels, and imagination plays dice with long-lasting sorrows: no one knows the name that trembles on the tip of my outer cervix's lips. The cancer patient is dead without having agreed to an operation, and the power of his fascination is gone with him to the morgue.

There will be much to say about the problems of fear and cancer. Cancer is linked to nightmares through the claws of the crab: the opacity of its cursed blossoming, the surprising way in which it solidifies fixed ideas, the aggressive bulimia of the little man. Yes, for me, cancer is indeed the son of nightmares, not the father.

I remember some of the verses that stumbled out of one of Byron's nuit blanches (*Childe Harold's Pilgrimage*, Canto IV, stanza 21):[32] "Existence may be borne, and the deep root of life and sufferance make its firm abode in bare and desolated bosoms: mute the camel labours with the heaviest load, and the wolf dies in silence."

32 A long, four-part narrative poem by the British poet Lord Byron (1788–1824) published between 1812–1818.

The cancer patient was buried in the garden of the red house that is at the northern end of the corniche. During the eulogy, read by Professor Muller, a fleet of small rubber dinghies—crewed by Copts of greenish complexion telling cruel jokes—pulled away from the dock and set sail in the direction of my youth. The sun's path, in essence.

Dreaming, I steadily climb the stairs that lead toward my house. The cornice snakes at my feet like a stream of urine, and there, the mist, called "clear skies," sprawls across Lausanne, the beautiful Levantine, in morning dress. The house, red at sunset, is ochre when seen from the lake against a backdrop of palm groves and blue sky.

S. and I buy the house after much effort and challenges: so many houses we visited, so many dreamlike connections cut to pieces, so much common ground surrendered to speculators. One of these houses supposedly belonged to the Conductor Almeida. I liked that house. Ronde-bosse sculpted wood panelling slathered in whitewash cluttered all the rooms from the floor to the ceiling; a collection of bird carcasses overflowed out of a broken window, and the dog of the former tenant was pecking at oat grains with the hens. "Should we buy it?" I asked, my throat filled with needles of joy, but the shadow of a cloud covered S.'s forehead.

"Many observations are, arguably, questionable," he said.

"What do you mean?"

"Something soft and opaque is hiding the landscape," said S., staring intently at the legs of an elderly lady who was passing by on the road. The woman, aware she was the target of our glances, bent over and loosened her girdle. Her buttocks exploded like a bomb in the calm afternoon. She fell into the ditch, revealing her whooping-cough crest, her velvet pubis, and all the substance of her unborn child still embedded in her flesh. "It's Barbarossa's old palace," laughed S., vulgar and thrilled.

Was it possible, I asked myself, that this harpy could be its only heir?

"Your evidence is a bit far-fetched," says S. in a vain effort of consolation: the old woman was upset that she might give birth to a monster.

"My child," she cried, "will be a squirrel!"

And when S. asked her what she was basing this fear on, she told him that, near the fifth month of her pregnancy, while she was walking in the woods, a squirrel had jumped on her shoulders and frightened her. "This is why my child will be redheaded," she said, lifting her skirts. S. and I approached and saw that the woman was telling the truth: the head of the unborn child had a good fortyish red hairs, but *only* fortyish...

"Sometimes even death smells of red embers," said S. sternly: he knows that in my dreams I have a soft spot for the redhead.

I liked the conductor's second house even more. "Only a balcony to jump over to see Boula Henein,"[33] declared S., sucking on his pipe.

I can clearly see the implications of these houses steeped in musical memories. The Africans claim there are three types of dreams:

1. The stupefying;
2. The prophetic;
3. The directed.

Will I lose the thread of my nights as well? The cycle of my thoughts often has square wheels. Five cycles are de-

33 The wife of Egyptian writer Georges Henein (1914–1973).

picted in Tintoretto's *Paradise*.[34] There are cycles on every road, and every road, sooner or later, leads to the hospital.

I awaken, agitated and frightened, after these dreams of domesticity. I go back to bed without knowing why I got up in the first place: the architecture of my brain, in somewhat poor taste, has always seemed solid, but now, at the slightest wink of the medical eye, the walls fall to their knees in a cloud of dust. I place the zero of my empty head on the pillow and retain *nothing*.

The shadow of the cancer patient floats upstream on the unknown beach. His bed is empty now. A heavy tightness weighs on the small group of visitors: they begin to understand that they are there less to please than to learn. A reserved, polite tone is required; one is ambitious without showing it, envious, and overly critical. The infection of the mood, excoriated by the vulgar germs of fear, is among the easiest. At the gate of sleep, death is standing, pensive; ahead of her run "goosebumps," behind her, the lagoon.

Although popular alive, the cancer patient's death saddened no one. Voluble and self-satisfied, he had no trouble convincing both doctors and patients of his decision to never be operated on at any cost. I still see him, playing cards with the addict, the bearded man, and my father in pyjama sleeves. The funeral ceremony began the night of Christmas Eve. "The unfortunate is 'dead by switchblade,'" said my father. The administration's efforts couldn't stop the news from spreading, and a strange thing, many of the bedridden experienced a sense of relief to see the matter so clearly cut. "Black is always dressy," said my father.

---

34 *Il Paradiso*: A large (22 x 9 metres) religious oil painting by Jacopo Robusti, more commonly known as Tintoretto (1518–1594), painted between 1588–1592.

Every day, around eleven o'clock, buckled into the colourful and indecisive uniform of a trout fisherman, the garçon of the floor, miraculously holding with his extended arm a tray crowded with cups of broth, walks by our filthy beds: "We must look at what the finger points to, not the pointed finger," he says, staring at the bearded man, the great navel-gazer. Rough gustatory images overtake the palate of the prone, and Mr. Cooper, legs and fly generously opened, his pink and grey penis caught between his index and middle fingers, wields his divining wand in a surprising manner.

"Hide your initials in front of the ladies, Mr. C.," says the floor garçon, smoothing his hair with his buttered hand. Mr. C., pausing his hands' intensive foraging, says, "I want to stress the first syllable of a lost word." Maybe he fears the hazards of solitude and the waves that hazard on these reefs? Seen from bed, Earth seems to be engulfed in the doorway: "The maternal intimacy of death," as told by Bachelard.[35]

"Probing question, probing question," laughs the garçon, gauche with happiness. "The opening does appear a little tight," concedes the Englishman, his face covered in shadow. "I remember now!" he says. "We say to 'coop up,' and that means 'to cage.'" "Cover yourself, Mr. C.," insists the garçon, linking the gesture to the image. "He must despise us only because he thinks every establishment across the Channel is a refuge for the useless and the timid: a sewer."

"Caca!" hurled Mr. Cooper, exasperated by the stupor of the bedridden crowd.

Exit the floor garçon.

Around noon, the mauve mood, associated with worry and nostalgia, falls flatly upon the Cantonal Hospital. It's time for the doctors' rounds. "There they are!" shouts the

35 Gaston Bachelard (1884–1962): French philosopher known for his work in poetics and in the philosophy of science.

bearded man from his bed near the elevator. The sick move and rotate to face the door. Fragments of ideas fly from head to head like melodies of the blind. It's time for the great denouement.

The men of science advance along the grand poplar avenue, between stone beds and those that look like tombs. "They're the dead, not us," mumbles the bearded man.

"Not so fast, not so fast," says an intern.

In France, popular folklore maintains that the dead are tied to the place of their death. The doctors strip, examine, talk, laugh. The nurses' dirty jokes catch in their throats. The chamber pots, previously commented on so nonchalantly, become obsolete. "The word is on the tip of the tongue"—Professor Muller's motto.

If we mention euthanasia to the Helvetii, their faces close like oysters. "The so-called assembly line 'of the dying' is the most inhumane manifestation of the capitalist world," says a Romanian visitor. "I'd rather suck off a dead man than a living one if the latter is a communist," says the mother of a widow-to-be.

"Even in death, I'll just be a machine?" says the addict in resignation.

"Caca," says my father, ever authoritarian.

"Deal," replies Professor Muller, removing the probe. He knows that the last thrill before death is found in the anus, that sink of the human body.

I remember M., the scatological spider who thought she was a nurse. "Everyone's a piece of shit," she would laugh, sprawled out on my grandparents' deathbed. Or, "The dead: the one and only lasting sustenance."

According to Frazer, "the uncivilized have all the same feelings for the dead that man has for the living." And vice versa?

I'm afraid. I rest in the dark among radiology machines and all kinds of refuse: projectiles or buds? Who knows? Too weak to hold a finger in each ear, I cry neither for the dead nor for the living. I wait.

Professor Muller's assistant has slyly approached my bed: he has screwed his large mouth to the crook of my ear, and pressing his tongue against my eardrum, he whistles as though to shape an *i*.

"Seriously, all this dreaming has you hearing nothing but Greek or Latin," says my father. A nurse yanks off the sheet and covers. Professor Muller leans against the wall, as if absent. "He really doesn't know where to start," says my father anxiously. But a strange rectal sensation, a taste of violet candy on the tip of my tongue, and a slight urge to vomit mean that all my orifices are now offered to the north wind's whims. This is why Ernest Jones thinks the fart is the source of the soul.

"Turn on the ceiling light," says Professor Muller. "I'm the one operating today."

"The world is upside down," says the Martinican, outraged by so much selfishness from a scientist.

I manage to turn on the ceiling light, and notwithstanding a violent bout of nausea, not unlike after swallowing consecutive doses of cod liver oil proffered from a filthy spoon, everything seems normal. I hear music in the next room, and I think about the English, held as prisoners in Gabon, who undoubtedly can no more write home than I can. In captivity, some ideas don't completely disappear but rather begin to shrink, change in appearance and direction, and end up stinking like the leftovers of a meal that has long since been forgotten.

"Perhaps I should consult another doctor?" says the man who is little more than a living corpse. Mine has taken my alarm clock: brave, piercing, and cheerful beast, the only irrefutable proof of my presence in the hospital. “Don’t worry, dear lady, we’ll meet again in your dreams,” he said as he left and closed the door without a single comforting word nor a promise of return. “Goodnight, ladies, it’s good to be alive,” were his final words in English. The last ones I heard before the Great Sleep.

The elevator door is locked. The elevator door looks like an icebox. Strange hospital, you say? Every key opens a different door but mine can only be opened with the force of my imagination… if at all.

No one knows the face of their own death. Mine has let her hair grow since the first day of the last night; her tears stream down her tetanus cheeks, and the horizon is no more than a giant wall of Gruyère. Slumber melts into avalanches, the bulimic eye swallows its own smoke, I turn my gaze inward and without hesitation or doubt recognize my mother's shadow. Beautiful, elegant, despite the mud on her dress and a bruised cheek, she signs the register in the office near the darkened window. As my father says to the addict on the nights of the full moon: "The end of the line."

I suppose I make a wrong move for the door. "It's no longer in your power to flee," says my mother nastily on her way to the mezzanine and to the joys of electroshock. "There's no need to rush. No need to hit the brakes..." "Why not?" I say through a vast, bloody yawn.

The red door with a black cross closes and closes again. All eyes are fixed on me with sadness and sympathy. "Because it's all or nothing," she says, as though curled up in her past, "Doctors, like gods, have no pity for the dreamers." Stunned by her insensitivity toward me and simultaneously mortified by the presence of two approximately twelve-year-old doctors, I don't know what to tell her or how to stop her from slipping stupidly toward dissolution.

My throat fills with a warm, sweet liquid. I spit. I drool. I drink, moving my mandibles, emptying my lungs, screaming: "I give up, I give up..." My throat fills again. You think my parents and friends are simply waiting for a sign to rush over? Sure, assuming there is someone behind the door... which I'm doubtful of. From the moment we accept the absurd isolation of the shrinking dark, the worst is almost over.

To sleep with an open belly, having willingly sacrificed the rocky shores of reason to the anglers. To sleep kneeling, like the tree of life: death is a freckle on the naked skull of the burning day. To sleep before the rock returns to the dust that it was. To listen to the gurgling of the snail who, having left its shell there on the path, leaves my mouth in corkscrews, in bubbles and ribbons: it's the thunder of desire that recedes.

"May her awakening be of roses," says the gravedigger.

TRANSLATOR'S ACKNOWLEDGEMENTS

I am grateful to the Haus der Kulturen der Welt in Berlin for inviting me to speak at the conference *Surreal Continuum* that first brought this project into focus, and for their generous support toward the publication of this book. I'm equally grateful to the Freie Universität Berlin for hosting me as a Dorothea Schlegel Artist-in-Residence with the Cluster of Excellence "Temporal Communities," where I was able to begin the translation.

I am deeply thankful to Norm at Invisible Books for embracing the book with such enthusiasm and supporting it from its earliest stages. My sincere appreciation goes to my editors, Mélissa Bull and Maxime Raymond Bock, whose deep dive into Mansour's play with language greatly strengthened the translation. I am also grateful to Cyrille Mansour for his support and encouragement and for kindly granting permission to reproduce Ted Joans' portrait of Joyce Mansour on the cover. I was fortunate to have the help of Andrea Miller-Nesbitt in tracking down countless library books and documents that proved invaluable during the research process. Finally, for a book begun in Berlin and finished in Montréal, I want to thank my village: the community whose curiosity, shared meals, and steady friendships carried me through this work.

Joyce Mansour (1928–1986) was born in England to a Jewish family of Syrian descent who moved to Egypt shortly after her birth, where she grew up among the English-speaking elite. After marrying a Francophone Egyptian, she learned to write in French and was exiled to Paris following the rise of Nasser. There, Mansour became one of the most uncompromising figures of the postwar Surrealist movement and the most significant poet to join the group after World War II. Indeed, she quickly became a close friend of André Breton and part of the movement's inner circle. She authored sixteen books of poetry, as well as prose works and plays, that confront desire, death, violence, and the female body with startling directness.

Emilie Moorhouse is a multidisciplinary writer, translator, and lecturer based in Montréal, Canada. Raised in a French-speaking household in Toronto, she holds an MFA from the University of British Columbia. Her writing has appeared in the *Globe and Mail,* the *Toronto Star,* and *PRISM International,* and she was a writer for two seasons of the TV show *Green Squad.* As a translator, her previous work includes *Emerald Wounds: Selected Poems of Joyce Mansour* (City Lights Books, 2023), which was longlisted for the 2024 Griffin Poetry Prize. Her decade-long involvement in the Canadian climate movement continues to inform and animate her creative and intellectual pursuits.

Invisible Books produces fine Canadian literature for those who enjoy such things. As an independent, not-for-profit publisher, we work to build communities that sustain and encourage engaging, literary, and current writing.

Called Invisible Publishing until 2026, Invisible Books has been in operation for nearly two decades. We released our first fiction titles in the spring of 2007, and our catalogue has come to include works of graphic fiction and nonfiction, pop culture biographies, experimental poetry, and prose.

We are committed to publishing writers with diverse perspectives. In acknowledging historical and systemic barriers, and the limits of our existing catalogue, we emphatically encourage writers from LGBTQ2SIA+ communities, Indigenous writers, and writers of colour to submit their work.

Invisible Books is also home to the Bibliophonic, Throwback, and DOCUMENTS series.